Lessons in Charm

JASMINE HARPER

Copyright © 2024 by Jasmine Harper.

The moral right of Jasmine Harper to be identified as the author of this work has been asserted in accordance with the Copyright Designs and Patents Act, 1988.

All rights reserved. No portion of this book may be reproduced or transmitted in any form or by any means, electronic or mechanical, including photocopy, recording, or any information storage and retrieval system, without written permission from the author.

This book is a work of fiction. Names, characters, businesses, organizations, places and events are either the product of the author's imagination or used fictitiously. Any resemblance to actual persons, living or dead, events or locales is entirely coincidental.

1

Our college campus looks more glamorous than it really is. An outside observer might admire the ornate Gothic stonework, medieval vaulted ceilings, dark wood panelling and intricate stained-glass windows built sometime back in the 1400s. The reality? A breathtaking place to study magic, but seriously bloody cold thanks to temperamental heating and an ornery caretaker who I swear has sadistic tendencies when it comes to keeping the place warm. There's a reason our uniform is mostly made of wool, and I feel sorry for those who are allergic to it.

Today, we're studying the laws of physics and how to bend them. And, as is always the way, Sara and I are struggling to focus. Instead, we're trying not to overtly perv on Mr Wakefield, the young and frustratingly handsome teacher.

"Is there a female equivalent to blue balls?" I whisper to Sara, who immediately starts to snigger. "Because if not, I blame the patriarchy."

"No, there is," she insists. "I heard someone refer to it as 'blue bean' once."

I swear I nearly die trying to suck in my laughter. I manage to remain silent, but I can feel my face turning red, and there's a tear dribbling down my right cheek. Sara has turned away from me, but I can see her shoulders shaking.

We're supposed to be finishing our practical write-ups in today's lesson, but it must be all too evident that we're not focusing on our work.

"Anything I can help with, Emilie?"

Mr Wakefield is suddenly beside me. I frantically wipe away the tear.

"No, sorry, just trying to contain my hiccups," I lie. "I was trying to be quiet."

God, I hope the rumours about him being telepathic aren't true. If they are, I'll have to fake my own death, leave England and start a new life in Tanzania.

He nods, seeming to understand my predicament, but I see a flicker of amusement flash across his face.

"Nearly done?" he asks.

"Nearly," I reassure him, and get back to my work.

I finish my essay. There's ten minutes of the lesson remaining, and I can see everyone else is hard at work, so I let my mind drift again. Rather than dipping into yet another fantasy about Mr Wakefield, this time I let my mind drift to my idyllic little stone cottage. In my daydreams, this is where I'll live one day.

I visualise the sage-green front door, the leafy climbers surrounding it, the subtle colour variations in the stone and the log burner in the lounge. One of my other teachers, who specialises in mindfulness and manifestation, encourages this kind of behaviour. Not the daydreaming in class I hasten to add, but visualising what we want on a regular basis. She refers to it as "sunbathing in our future" and says that if we don't allow ourselves to think about what we really want, our brains won't look for opportunities to make it happen. Perhaps I could use this theory to excuse my filthy fantasies about Mr Wakefield.

I sneak a look at him. He's turned away from me, bent forward to look at something on his desk. I admire his jaw, the flop of his hair, his delicious forearm, the way his fingers are splayed on the desk as he looks over something. God, it's almost too much.

I feel bad for objectifying him, I really do. But, truthfully, it's not just a shallow physical thing – I wouldn't find him at all attractive if he was an arsehole. Sadly, he isn't; he's a really kind, emotionally intelligent guy who seems to sense the mood of the class and tailor his lessons accordingly. He is universally adored, and I find my mind wandering yet again as I imagine what it would be like to kiss him.

Just as I'm contemplating how much tongue is too much tongue, Mr Wakefield catches my eye and smiles. I understand this is to acknowledge that I've finished my work and am waiting patiently for others to do the same, but my raging libido takes this to mean something else entirely. Blue bean, indeed.

The bell rings, the sound slicing through the silence. Mr Wakefield instructs us to leave our work on our desks, and there's a flurry of activity as everyone gets to their feet. As the class files slowly towards the door, I steal another glance at him.

His head is bowed as he collects our essays, but as I pretend to straighten my uniform to buy myself a second more ogling time, he looks up at me, one eyebrow raised. Naturally I panic, nearly tripping over myself as I turn to follow the rest of the class, who are now spilling out into the corridor.

Out of his line of sight, disaster narrowly averted, I berate myself. This cannot continue. I run the risk of humiliating myself if I don't get a grip. I promise myself that, somehow, I will find a way to get some alone time tonight and relieve some of the tension.

When I hear Eleanor's gentle snoring, that's when I know I don't have to wait any longer. But before I climb out of bed, I focus again, listening to the breathing of the others. It is slow, heavy; they are in a deep sleep. Silently, I slip out from under the covers and pull on my slippers – celestial-patterned faux-fur-lined booties – wrap the heavy black cloak around my shoulders and creep quietly out of the room. As soon as I enter the corridor, I feel a wave of relief, a relaxing in the pit of my stomach. Not from having successfully escaped, although that is certainly part of it, but from finally being alone.

The problem with boarding school is that you're always in company. Privacy is a rare thing. At night, you're sharing a room with five others. The showers are in such high demand that you can't afford to be in them a moment longer than necessary, for fear of making someone late for class. For an introvert and people-pleaser like me, that's hard. And it's even harder when you're eighteen and have spent Friday afternoon with the devastatingly handsome Mr Wakefield. I know it's a cliché to have a crush on a teacher, and I used to berate myself for it, but when I discovered that he was just five years older than me, that crush somehow became easier to justify. Nothing wildly inappropriate about that... right? Look, just humour me here.

Impatient, I force myself to slow down, not wanting to trip. I know exactly where I'm going – the observatory. Luckily, I know this campus so well that it's easy to navigate in the dark; just the dim yellow glow from the lamps outside light my way.

I find the door and open it. The staircase is a narrow, steep spiral, so I reach for the rope on the side of the wall and start to count the steps, ignoring the thoughts urging me to focus on how bloody claustrophobic this bit of the journey is. Two hundred steps, and then I'll be at the top, and I already know it'll be worth it.

My slippers are silent on the staircase. My legs are bare, but I'm not cold. I'm only wearing short cotton pyjamas, but the heavy cloak pulled around me is all the protection I need from the plunging night-time temperatures.

I reach the top and nearly groan in delight as I look out of the vast windows that overlook the playing fields. The stars are so clear and bright, I can even make out the Milky Way. It is so quiet up here, I am so *alone* and I couldn't be happier. It is closing in on midnight; everyone is asleep. Tomorrow is Saturday so I'll have the opportunity to lie in. I've been looking forward to this all week, and I quite literally hug myself in delight.

In the starlight, I can just discern the outlines of the furniture in the room, the various jars and bottles, and the telescope by the window. There are bookshelves, a handful of desks and, beside the biggest window, a sofa. It's low to the ground and covered in a big velvet throw. I walk over and drop onto it, throwing my head back so it rests on the sofa. Bliss. I spread my arms and legs wide like a starfish, sinking deeper into the soft cushions, and let my eyes scan the sky. I can see the skeletal outline of trees on the horizon, and then the stars, the Milky Way; like someone's knocked over a tube of silver glitter onto black sugar paper.

I take in a long, deep, full breath and begin to undo the buttons of my broderie pyjama top. I'm naked underneath, of course. I feel the cool air on my breasts, and my nipples harden. I'm already wet.

I let my focus soften, and I think of Mr Wakefield. What would he think if he knew I was here, fantasising about him and about to make myself come imagining him doing the same? He'd be horrified, probably. But I try not to let this ruin what's going to be the most-needed orgasm in history.

My mind searches for an image. Rather than fabricate another fantasy, I find myself recalling one of my favourite memories, something that actually occurred a few months ago.

It happened when I was speed-walking to my next lesson, late yet again, the campus deserted with everyone in class.

One minute I'm walk-running, the next I'm falling through the air, my cloak flying out behind me. I'm aware of the sheer velocity of the fall, wind whistling through my hair as I hurtle onto the concrete path.

I'm dazed, and it takes me a moment to realise what's happened. I've fallen – tripped over myself, in fact. What a clutz.

I don't register the pain immediately. I look at my bloodied palms, and it's only when I see the bright-red grazes that I feel the sharp sting. Tentatively, I attempt to climb to my feet without putting weight on my hands and realise I must have sprained an ankle because a javelin of pain assaults me as I try to put weight on my right foot.

I'm what feels like miles from the nearest building. There's no one around; everyone is in a lesson. Tears of self-pity threaten as the pain begins to build, and I try to pull myself together so I can figure out what to do about this fun new situation I find myself in.

Just as I'm thinking I might very well die here, cold and alone, I see a figure rushing towards me. Despite being some distance away, I recognise him immediately.

Mr Wakefield.

By the time he reaches me, I'm sat in a crumpled pile on the path, legs crooked, bloodied palms face up in my lap.

He stops an appropriate distance away, about a metre from me.

"I saw you fall," he says, looking pained. "Can you get up?"

"I tried." I can hear the defeat in my voice. "I think I've sprained my ankle."

He hesitates for just a second. "Could you stand on one leg if I helped you up?"

"I think so…" I say, but I'm not at all confident. Plus, the thought of hopping a considerable distance back to the main building fills me with dread.

"I'll support your arms if you can balance on your good foot. I'll pull you up..."

Anxiety must be written all over my face. The potential for disaster is huge. I twist myself into position, and he kneels in front of me, taking hold of my elbows.

His face is inches from mine, concern etched all over it. "Ready?"

My heart all but stops. "Yup," I squeak, my voice at least two octaves higher than before.

This man is deceptively strong. He pulls me up with so much force I end up falling forward, and it's only my hands on his biceps that stop me from crashing into him.

We eye each other, looking to see how the other will respond.

"Made it," I say, starting to giggle.

He's smiling. "Now we just need to get you inside."

He turns to look at the long stretch of path ahead of us and exhales. "Okay. Put your arm around my shoulder. I'll support your body."

Turns out that involves him wrapping an arm around my waist and pinning me against him while I hobble back into the school. I'm convinced I've died and gone to heaven; RIP me. The jarring pain in my ankle, my bloody hands, the inconvenience of crutches will all be worth it for these fleeting moments pressed up against Mr Wakefield.

"Any chance of a piggyback?" I tease, only half-joking. This would be so much easier if he could just sweep me up in his arms and carry me inside. He laughs, and I feel it rumble in his chest, which is pressed against my side. Even in my pain I'm cataloguing every last detail to recount to Sara later.

We make it into the building. It's hard work, and by the time I get there, I'm sweating. We enter an empty classroom, and Mr Wakefield eases me gently into a chair. The relief of no longer having to stand is quickly replaced by anguish as he releases me.

"I'll go find the nurse."

He leaves the room. I catch sight of myself in a glass-fronted cabinet and notice I look slightly crazed; my hair, the colour of weak tea, is escaping from the updo I attempted this morning.

Moments later, Mr Wakefield returns with a wheelchair, looking sheepish, and parks it beside me.

"I'm sorry, I didn't realise we had one. The nurse apparently has to hide it because her last one kept getting stolen, and she suspected the teachers were responsible." The way he looks at me, a grin dancing on his face, tells me I've been let in on a delicious in-joke.

"Shall I help you into it?"

"Please."

He leans down then and, without warning, scoops me up and hugs me to him as he transfers me carefully into the wheelchair.

"Okay?" he asks, seeing my surprise as he straightens up. He looks rather surprised himself.

I simply nod in reply, not trusting my voice, my heart hammering like a drum in my chest. I start to wonder if this is one of those lucid dreams Eleanor's been telling me about. Then

Mr Wakefield wheels me into the empty corridor and we're off. It's just the two of us and the squeak of the secret wheelchair.

"Did you have much planned for the weekend?"

"Oh, you know. Football, roller skating, a ballet lesson," I joke, trying to make him laugh.

I'm rewarded with a chuckle. "You might have to reconsider. That was a spectacular fall."

I notice the subtlest change in Mr Wakefield's demeanour as he wheels me into the nurse's office.

She greets me with a question: "What do we have here then?"

"A sprained ankle, I think," I tell her.

She nods abruptly, her bullshit-detector satisfied. "You're also bleeding," she says, motioning to my hands, and immediately I twist in my seat to look at Mr Wakefield's pristine white shirt. As far as I can tell, it's miraculously still pristine.

He smiles so warmly at me then, as if amused by the reason for my panic, and my stomach plummets as his brown eyes meet mine, my sprained ankle suddenly far from my mind.

"I can take it from here, Mr Wakefield," the nurse says firmly.

"Of course," he says, and in my fantasies, that hint of embarrassment I detect, his half-beat of hesitation, is related to the fact that he doesn't want to leave. I know that can't be true, but there's no harm in pretending – or so I tell myself.

"I hope you recover quickly, Emilie," he says with a final glance before swiftly exiting the room.

I close my eyes now, remembering the way his warm body felt against mine, his pine-and-patchouli shower gel, the curve of his biceps. I remember his devastating smile in the nurse's office, how being the recipient of such a rare gift feels like a lottery win.

With the memory of his body still so fresh in my mind, it's all too easy to imagine how things could have taken a turn for the hotter; where things might have led had he abandoned all sense of professionalism. How, instead of the nurse's office, he could have carried me into my empty dorm and tended to me on my bed...

I slide my hand into my knickers. It's a veritable flood down there. I'm probably kidding myself if I think one orgasm will suffice. I'll need at least three before I can leave here satisfied.

I pull my shorts and knickers off, leaving them in a small heap on the floor. Spreading my legs wider, I arch my back and try not to rush. I could come in less than a minute, but I don't want to. I want to enjoy every second of this. I cup myself, the wetness, and begin to massage myself with my palm.

The sound makes me freeze. I go from unadulterated bliss to pure terror in less than a second. I turn my head a fraction, and there he is.

I wish for death, instant and complete.

Mr Wakefield is standing three metres away, his jaw on the floor.

Fuck.

2

I can't speak; I'm trembling violently. Why the fuck is he here? Immediately, the consequences of this "incident" run through my mind: I'll be a laughing stock, I'll have to leave this college, my parents will be furious. And they'll be sickened to find out why. Fuck my life.

So when he says, "I'm so sorry, Emilie; I didn't mean to disturb you," I burst into tears – big, ugly, heaving sobs. I turn away from him and face the wall, trying to stem the flow with the corner of my cloak, which is now hastily wrapped around me. It is, of course, hopeless.

"I just wanted some fucking privacy," I manage to choke out. "Just half an hour to myself. I'm never alone in this fucking place."

His voice is shaky and low. "I understand. I'm so sorry. I came up here for some peace and quiet myself. I had no idea..." He trails off. He had no idea some sixth former would be up here masturbating.

I fantasise about jumping out of the window. We're so high up, death would be guaranteed. But he would probably be scarred for life, traumatised. He'd have to give up teaching, would gradually retreat into himself, mute and permanently damaged by the image of my brains splattered across the cobblestones below. Burning humiliation and banishment for me it is, then.

"I won't tell anyone," he says. "You just wanted some privacy. There's nothing wrong with that."

I manage to turn towards him and force myself to look at his face. His expression is anguished. I'm struggling to comprehend this – why does he look so guilty when I was the one in the wrong? I'm supposed to be in bed asleep, not having orgasms in the observatory.

A single crystal tumbler on the worktop nearest him catches my attention. Beside it sits a bottle of golden liquid with a cork stopper. So that was the sound – glass bottle meeting wooden counter – that I heard.

I slump back against the sofa. Despite his reassurances, I'm still trembling.

"Are you cold?" he asks.

"No. It's just shock." I glance at him out the corner of my eye. He's wringing his hands together, clearly anxious. I've never seen him like this before.

I look down at myself, wrapped in a black woollen cloak, bare legs poking out from beneath it, my ridiculous slipper boots on my feet.

"Can I get you something? Or... I should go, shouldn't I? Do you want me to go?"

I don't answer. Honestly, I don't know what to say. He's featured in my fantasies so frequently but, my God, the shock of actually seeing him here when I'm almost naked... I wonder why he's loitering. Perhaps he's worried about me. I am still shaking, albeit less violently than a few minutes ago.

"I'm leaving," he says, and my head snaps up so I'm looking at him. "As in—" He actually laughs. "As in, leaving the school. In two weeks. It'll be announced in assembly on Monday."

Now it's my turn to gawp, open-mouthed, at him. I register my emotions: shock, disappointment, surprise.

"So I hope that's of some comfort," he continues. "I mean it when I say I won't tell anyone. I understand the need for privacy in this place. You weren't doing anything wrong. Not morally wrong. You know I've never cared too much about the arbitrary rules in this place."

With my cloak still pulled around me I look like some sort of odd caterpillar. I shift so I'm sitting upright.

"I'm..." I'm sorry to hear that? Is that even the appropriate thing to say now? Instead, my curiosity gets the better of me. "Where are you going?" I ask instead.

He mentions the name of a college I've never heard of. "Better pay, more responsibility. I'm ready for a new challenge," he says.

My cloak starts to slip, and as I try to surreptitiously adjust it, his expression suddenly changes. "God, I'm sorry. I'm intruding. I should go, shouldn't I?"

I find my voice. "Do you have any alcohol?" I ask, my gaze coming to land on the bottle of golden liquid next to him. The shaking has slowed, but I'm still trembling.

He smiles, a shy grin that reaches his eyes. My stomach plummets, and I think about the fact that, only moments ago, he saw me pleasuring myself. Good God.

To my surprise, he walks over to the bottle, pours some of the amber liquid into the glass then turns and hands it to me.

Seeing my amazement, he says, "You're not the only one who likes to spend time up here."

I allow myself a small smile. "I see."

He nods at the glass, expectant. "Try it."

I do. I'm not sure what I was expecting – something peaty and unpleasant, I suppose, medicinal perhaps – but this isn't. It smells, in fact, like the sea, and I'm immediately reminded of my favourite beach. I wonder if it's enchanted.

When the liquid hits my tongue, I taste that it's sweet, but also salty and warming. I'm reminded of molten caramel. How unexpected.

"It's actually rum," he tells me. "Tidal rum." He walks over and picks up the bottle. "Infused with Pepper Dulse seaweed, foraged at low tide during a full moon."

"Shit, this is... good. It's amazing, in fact."

"Isn't it."

I hold the glass up and study the liquid, swirling it round in the glass. "Is it enchanted?"

"No. Just great rum."

I notice I've stopped shaking. I've also stopped catastrophising. Perhaps I won't end up leaving, excommunicated and disgraced. Perhaps it'll be okay. I almost can't believe he's being so cool about this. Almost.

"This is helping," I tell him, feeling the warmth hit my veins and my brain drop into a marginally more relaxed state. Alcohol is impossible to get hold of here. It's technically banned, although I've always suspected the teachers still have it. Turns out, I was right.

"So you come up here, too?" I muse aloud, more to myself than anything. How funny. It's surprising that we haven't bumped into each other before now then, that being the case.

He nods.

"Although perhaps not for the same reason I do..." I say, and immediately I wonder why the fuck I'm bringing the conversation back to that when he'd so graciously let me off the hook.

He blushes, smiles, looks at the floor.

"Sorry, that was an utterly inappropriate thing to say. I have no idea why I'm bringing the conversation back round to that. You *should* report me; I'm an idiot." My cheeks are burning, and it's my turn to avoid eye contact.

My gaze falls on the small pile of clothes on the floor – my knickers and pyjama shorts. Fuck, I'd forgotten about those. Did he see them?

When I look back at his face, I can tell that he has – he followed my gaze, and now his struggles are writ large on his face. He's fighting with himself, trying not to laugh. I'm fighting with the urge not to jump out of the window. I stretch out my leg and kick my clothes back under the sofa so they're at least out of sight.

"I didn't think anyone was going to be up here," I all but groan, squeezing my eyes shut as I feel the familiar prickle of tears.

"Emilie, please believe me when I say it's fine."

"Will you get your own room in your new job?"

He laughs, runs a quick hand through his hair. "Yes."

"Well thank fuck for that, eh?" I say, downing what's left in the glass.

"Quite. Want another?"

I shake my head. I haven't had alcohol since I returned home months ago. It's gone straight to my head. I'm already dreading the prospect of descending those bloody stairs whilst inebriated.

"Are you not having one?" I ask, wondering why he hasn't poured one for himself.

He smiles, shakes his head. "Only one glass."

Hmm. Only one glass. He's always up here alone. So he's... single? Perhaps. He's probably not dating someone here, but he could have some long-distance, devastatingly beautiful girlfriend.

I put the glass down on the floor and, as I lean back again, I catch a whiff of myself. I smell, unmistakably, of sex. This situation is insane. And about to get awkward; now that I've finished my drink, there's no reason for us to be here. But I don't want to navigate The Stairwell of Death just yet.

He's been standing all this time, and I only notice this because he pulls up a stool and sits on it. He's not planning on going anywhere either, then. It strikes me that he could have sat on the sofa next to me but didn't. I appreciate the gesture, even though I wouldn't have minded.

"Emilie, I want to ask you a question. But it's not something a teacher should really ask a student."

I feel my eyebrows hit my hairline. I make an effort to keep my voice steady. "Okay."

But he remains quiet, like he needs more encouragement.

"Mr Wakefield—" I start.

"Tom," he insists.

"Tom." God, that feels weird. I knew his Christian name, of course, but this has to be the first time I've ever spoken it aloud.

"Tom," I continue, "you've been incredibly... gracious. The least I can do is allow you to ask a question."

"You don't know what the question is yet."

"Okay, well, that's fair. Fine, I promise to give you the benefit of the doubt."

He nods, his lips pursed as though he's trying to decide whether to ask.

"Do you have... a boyfriend? Or a girlfriend?"

Wow. Not at all what I was expecting him to say. I attempt to hide my surprise with a laugh. "No boyfriend. It's been a while since I had one of those, as is surely obvious from... well."

He fights a grin.

Feeling bolstered by his question, I ask the same. "You?"

"No girlfriend. There's not exactly a plethora of viable options here. Not unless I want to lose my job. And even if I was willing to take that risk... well, it's morally wrong."

"You've never magicked yourself a temporary one? For the sake of... scratching an itch?" He has access to that level of complex magic. I don't.

His shoulders shake as he laughs. "No," he manages, unable to contain his mirth. "Never. I'm not sure how I feel about that. Besides, you know it would backfire."

"It would if I tried it. But I reckon I'm about desperate enough to try. It's lucky I can't."

Together, we laugh. Then, slowly, the laughter subsides.

"We should go," I say.

"We should," he replies.

But neither of us move.

"You deserve someone lovely, Emilie," he says suddenly, and I can't believe the words are coming out of his mouth. "You're funny and witty and beautiful. Don't settle, don't compromise. Hold out for someone worthwhile. Honest, good. Loyal."

I'm stunned. His expression is earnest, sincere. It's almost like he's pleading with me.

"That's a really kind thing to say," I manage. "Thank you."

He stands suddenly; walks over to the bottle of rum. I'm still reeling. Christ. I wasn't expecting that.

"Would you like another drink?" He suddenly stiffens. "Oh God, I'm not trying to get you drunk. I just..." He groans.

There it is, that blush again. Even in the dark I can see it, his face illuminated only by the starlight and a tiny sliver of moon. He turns so he's facing away from me.

It's my turn to reassure him, now. "It's fine," I say. "Really."

He turns back to face me. God, he's gorgeous. I know I shouldn't think it, but... sweet Jesus. He's cupping his chin in his hand, a thoughtful if slightly pained expression on his face.

"Yes, please. I will have another drink, if you're offering."

He looks surprised. "Are you sure?"

"Yes, it's delicious. Thank you."

He pours me another; hands me back the glass. As he does, our hands touch. It takes every ounce of mental strength to hide my reaction.

He sits down on the stool again, and again I'm struck by his pained expression.

"Are you okay?"

He nods, but it's clear he isn't. "I should probably go."

"I understand."

I'm not keeping him here. I take a sip of the delicious, sweet, salty, warming liquid and groan a little. "This is so good."

He looks up then; smiles. The way his hair is all tousled from where he's been fidgeting with it... I actually have to look away. I focus on the stars, the Milky Way splashed obscenely across the sky.

"Beautiful, isn't it?" he says, as if he's read my mind.

It occurs to me then that I have a question for him, but even with a fair bit of alcohol in me, I'm hesitant. Legend has it that Mr Wakefield – Tom – is telepathic. And it's one of those rumours that seems silly at first – telepathy is so rare, even among those who study magic – but he always seems so in tune with the mood of the class, always so compassionate and kind, that it wouldn't be entirely out of the question.

"Can I ask you something?" I venture. The alcohol is making me brave.

He nods, and it's almost as though he knows what I'm going to ask him. How ironic.

"There's a rumour going round. That you're... telepathic. That you can read our thoughts. Is that true?"

He closes his eyes, his brow furrowed, and sighs. It's an age before he opens his eyes again. Finally, he speaks.

"Yes, it's true."

3

I try to hide my shock. I fail, utterly speechless. I really didn't think the rumour was true. The implications start to sink in, and my heart races, nausea rolling in my gut. I don't need to say a word; I'm horrified and he knows it. Silence hangs in the air. I have an overwhelming urge to laugh or cry, maybe both. It's like finding out your parents have read your diary. But worse.

"So…" I choke out.

"So…"

"You know."

"About?"

That I have a stonking great crush on you, I think.

"Oh," he says. Evidently, he heard that.

"I can't be the only one."

"You're not. God, I sound arrogant. I don't mean it like that. But, you know… a school full of sexually frustrated teenage girls… I don't take it personally. I'm just an outlet."

You're also utterly gorgeous, I think and then remember he can hear me. Fuck. This is impossible.

He answers the question I'm pondering before the thought has even fully formed. "Sometimes I can block out other people's thoughts," he tells me. "But not always... If I'm tired, it's especially difficult. So I did know... how you felt," he falters.

Even in the dark I can tell he's blushing again.

He continues. "I'm sure you can understand why I didn't want people knowing I have this power. Believe me when I say it's a curse far more than it is a blessing."

He looks defeated, and my heart goes out to him. It's only when you think about the real implications of having such a power, truly, that you realise just how much of a burden it could be.

Unable to stop myself, I think back to some of the inappropriate thoughts I've had about him. The way I've admired the delicious curve of his bottom in class, or, worse, so much worse, how I'd imagine myself on my knees, classroom suddenly empty, taking the full length of him in my mouth. And I realise I'm not sure what's worse – him walking in on me masturbating, or him knowing my innermost, filthiest, most objectifying thoughts.

I dare myself to meet his gaze, knowing he'll have heard all that. He's wearing a pained expression, his eyes closed. Did he manage to block those ones out?

"You're wondering just how many of your thoughts I've heard over the years," he says. It's not a question. It doesn't need to be.

I nod.

"I want you to know I really did try to block them out. Because it felt like such an invasion of your privacy. But I did hear some."

I laugh. I can't help myself. This is such a dire situation.

"By some do you mean...?"

He nods. "You have a vivid imagination," he says, and I think I see the tiniest glimpse of a smile.

I put my head in my hands, momentarily forgetting that I'm not wearing much beneath my cloak. I panic as it starts to slide, quickly pulling it around myself again, a clumsy little black caterpillar.

It all makes sense. His compassion, his understanding when he found me up here on my own. He understands me so much better than I ever imagined because, whether he wanted it or not, he's had access to my most private thoughts.

My legs are shaking again. I down a big mouthful of the rum. I already have my plan for tomorrow mapped out. Stay in bed, hungover and tired, and blame it on my period. God, I'm struggling to process this, what it means. I'm struck by how one-sided it is.

"It is unfair," he says, quite literally reading my thoughts. "You can ask me anything you want to. I'll do my best to answer, in a bid to even things out a bit."

What an invitation. There's nothing I don't want to know. Never in a million years did I think I'd have this opportunity. My curiosity overrides my fear.

"Have you ever had a crush on anyone here?"

He's silent, and I can't read his expression.

When he continues to say nothing, I press him. "You've never had a crush on a pupil here, have you?"

"I've never willingly had a crush on a pupil here."

"What does that mean?"

"Oh, Emilie. You know what that means." He reaches out to take my now-empty glass from me.

I don't. At least not immediately. The alcohol is making my cognition slow. Okay, so he's never willingly had a crush on a pupil here... which means... which means he *has* had a crush on someone here. Finally. Got it.

Instead of addressing that thought, he says, "You're tired, aren't you?" His voice is soft, kind, and my insides melt. It's not a voice he uses often. Mostly we get his confident, assertive-teacher voice; occasionally his sarcastic, acid-tipped tone when he's employing a biting quip to keep a disorderly pupil in line.

"A bit. It's the alcohol more than anything."

"Are you warm enough?"

"Do you need to ask?"

He laughs at that.

"Who is she?"

He abruptly stops laughing. His face falls, and I instantly regret opening my mouth.

"I'm sorry. Look, you don't have to tell me. Instead, you could tell me what she's like. Describe her to me. If that's less harrowing."

He nods, his face set, grim. I wonder why he offered to answer my questions when he appears so reluctant. Besides, only moments ago, he asked me if I was single.

"I know you think I'm a hypocrite," he starts, "but this isn't just about having a crush on someone. It's about having a crush on someone you really shouldn't. Because, you know, my job."

"I get that."

"Okay. Good."

He starts pacing the room. "You want me to describe her?"

"I do. If you don't mind."

"So here's the thing. When you're telepathic, you get to know people so much better for being able to hear all that internal chatter. So although she's outwardly beautiful, I also happen to know she's a really kind-hearted person. It's weird, it's a crush, but it's deeper simply because I'm privy – in a way I feel horrendously guilty about, I might add – to her thoughts."

"That's... really interesting. So, by default, all your crushes will be more than superficial feelings based on someone's appearance because you're able to get to know that person without even talking to them?"

"Exactly that."

"Huh. That's pretty cool."

He shakes his head. "If it wasn't so risky, I'd have the power removed. But I'm not willing to risk my life. Anyway."

"Anyway," I mirror. I'm desperate for a name still. And trying not to feel jealous. He would know, and jealousy is so unbecoming.

"I know you're desperate for a name," he says. He stands, walks over to me and picks up the glass I've been using. Fetching the bottle, he pours himself a finger of rum and downs it immediately.

"That's a waste of delicious rum."

"I wouldn't say so. Not now I know how desperate you are for a name."

"You'll give it to me?"

"Do I need to?"

"What does that mean?"

"Emilie," he sighs, his tone bordering on frustrated as he pours himself another drink.

The penny drops. Or, at least, I think it does. But I want to be sure because this seems... unlikely. In fact, so unlikely that I'm beginning to think I'm in my dorm, asleep, dreaming all this up.

"Me?" It's impossible to keep the incredulity from my voice.

"Yes. You."

It's as though someone has cast a spell on me, as though I'm frozen solid. I can't move; I'm speechless. Someone else would have seen this coming. I, however, didn't. I blame the rum.

A thought occurs. "Is this why you're leaving?" I manage.

"Not entirely. But it's a bonus. If that's the right word? Gives me the opportunity to try and... forget."

Ouch. I don't want to be forgotten. I didn't know he thought of me like that, but now I know, I don't want to be banished from his mind so soon. He can, of course, hear all this, and we both know it. We sit in silence. And then I have an idea. It's grossly unfair, of course, but I'm feeling rejected and sore and, I suppose if I'm honest, desperate. Because, more than ever, I don't want him to leave.

So I stare out at the night sky and imagine him walking over to me, unbuttoning his trousers and allowing me to take his delicious cock in my mouth. In my mind, I start to suck. I hear groaning. It's coming from real-life Tom.

"Emilie," he says.

It's not clear whether he wants me to stop. He doesn't tell me to, explicitly at least, so I carry on. I'm licking the tip, allowing myself to taste the clear liquid that's appeared there.

"Stop," he says, his voice a whisper. And I do, worried I've been anything but kind-hearted.

"I'm sorry."

He turns away from me. I feel awful.

"I don't want some sordid affair with a pupil," he says, running his hand through his hair again in the way he does when he's agitated. "I want... a proper girlfriend. To go on dates. To be able to tell everyone about us. I don't want any secrets. I don't want a relationship shrouded in shame."

Wow. I had no idea he felt that way.

"Me too," I admit. "But I also, right now, want your mouth between my legs." And I do. So badly. I don't care anymore.

He doubles over as if winded, his hand gripping the counter he's standing beside. "Emilie, you know it would be wrong."

He's right – of course he is. Morally reprehensible, probably illegal. But I still feel the sting of rejection. Is it that bad? Really? I'm not an underage schoolkid; I'm an adult, albeit a young one, two years over the age of consent. I'm a sixth former. A student, not a pupil. Surely that changes things?

It doesn't, of course. And what's also relevant here is how he feels about it. Plus, if I'm being entirely fair, it would matter a great deal if the head found out. I feel my insides shrivel with disappointment. He's right. This is impossible.

"I'm sorry," I whisper. "I'm being incredibly unfair. I'll be fine after an orgasm or twenty."

I'm making light of it, but I'm aware of an unfamiliar sensation in my chest. It's how I imagine a broken heart would feel. A heavy, crushing sensation right behind my breastbone.

But then he's beside me, on his knees in front of me. And he begins to slowly, so slowly, open my cloak to expose my thighs, unwrapping me as though I'm a gift. He's giving me every opportunity to say no. And there is absolutely no fucking way I will.

"You are the most beautiful woman I've ever laid eyes on," he says, his voice cracking. He's wearing the most ridiculously intense expression, his eyes huge and soft.

I part my legs for him, and the cloak slides off my lap. His gaze drops, then his eyes are back on mine again. He looks like he's in some kind of physical pain. I'm on the brink of coming. One touch – that's all it's going to take.

Please, I think. I plead with him. I can see his breathing is laboured. And, thanks to the way the light is coming in through the window, I can see the shadow of something huge straining against the zip of his trousers.

He rests his hands on my thighs, caressing them, and then he bows his head and kisses me.

4

I explode. I'm coming – so loudly I can't help it – only vaguely aware that I'm pulling his hair and bucking my hips, pushing myself against his mouth.

I come for what feels like a full minute – is that even humanly possible? – and fall back onto the sofa, delirious.

"Oh my God, you taste so good," he pants. His pupils are huge, intoxicated, his lips shiny and slick.

My legs are trembling. The words "best orgasm of my entire life" drift through my consciousness.

He laughs. "I didn't do much."

"Oh, on the contrary," I reply, still struggling to catch my breath. "You were a key player. This is the culmination of years of fantasising."

He grins. "You're not wrong. God, the stories I could tell you about the times you nearly derailed a lesson with your lascivious thoughts."

"Please, tell me more," I beg. God damn, I want to know Every. Last. Fucking. Detail.

"When you're sat at your desk thinking that stuff, it's like I can see it play out before me in 3D. Your imagination is *so* vivid. Some days I down a coffee before our lessons just so I stand a chance of blocking some of it out."

"So coffee's your kryptonite?"

"No, it's the opposite, really. It gives me an alertness I can use to bat other people's thoughts away. I'm usually buoyed up on caffeine in your lessons. It's the only way I can hope to get through an entire hour with you. It's always such a relief when you eventually decide to focus on what I'm actually saying."

He's on the sofa beside me now, pulling me towards him so that I land in his arms. He cups my face and kisses my cheek. "You've been a thorn in my side the entire time I've known you."

I must look delighted because he laughs. "Emilie," he says.

I love the way he says my name, with a hint of a French accent. It's sexy as hell. Then he closes his eyes, as if remembering just how incredibly risky and stupid this is.

"This is madness," he groans.

"I know," I groan back.

I notice his pained expression has returned. I want to smooth it away, to have a few more moments of uninhibited, delicious sexy time with this man.

"It's just so wild that you know all of my fantasies."

"The ones I didn't manage to bat away, yes."

"What's your favourite?"

"Impossible to pick. But there is one that particularly stands out in my mind, because you nearly cost me my job."

"*What?*"

"I'd had a late night and was running behind before a class so had no time to find coffee. Worst possible state to find myself in for a lesson with you."

"Which lesson was this?"

"I can't remember exactly what I was teaching that day, but I remember the brilliant sunshine. You asked to move desks because you were being blinded, and you sat right at the front of the class. I could have cried."

"I remember that day! It was just before the Easter break."

"I don't remember the lesson, but I remember exactly what you were thinking."

"Tell me."

"You don't remember?"

"I do, but I want to hear you describe it."

"You're awful."

"Oh, I am. But you already know that."

"It was a particularly kinky day for you."

I snort. "Must have been ovulating."

He laughs. "I know more than I ever imagined I would about the menstrual cycle after working at an all-girls school."

"I bet. Continue."

"You were imagining yourself bent over your desk, still dressed in uniform but no knickers. In your fantasy, I'd bound your hands and blindfolded you, very gently of course..." He stops when he catches sight of the expression on my face, my disbelief.

"Are you okay?"

"God, of course you know how I like to be touched..." I shake my head. This is wild. I'm struggling to fully comprehend the extent of his... gift. "You know almost all of my fantasies – the ones you didn't manage to block, anyway. And all my preferences..."

It suddenly strikes me then, in that moment, that this man is going to be the best fuck of my life. It takes all my willpower not to strip right there and then and straddle his lap. He's laughing so hard that the sofa is moving and tears are forming in his eyes. He wipes them away. I don't know what to say. A grin is plastered on my face.

"You look a bit like you've won the lottery," he says.

"I feel like I've won the lottery," I reply. "Please carry on – I'm dying to know what happens."

"Okay, so you were imagining me, er... I was behind you, one hand gently pulling your plait as I—" He swallows, suddenly hesitant. "It was... a bit much."

"Uh-huh." I am literally having the time of my life, listening to him recall this.

"And, as I'm sat at my desk at the front of the class, it becomes apparent that I have... a problem to deal with. And that the problem needs to be dealt with before it... escalates."

"Escalates?" I repeat.

"Yes. So I tell the class to do some reading, which probably seems a bit sudden, but everyone's rather distracted, especially you, so I take advantage of this and go into the store cupboard behind the blackboard."

"And...?"

"Oh, come on, Emilie," he chides gently. "I'm sure if anyone can figure that out, it's you. I've never felt so grubby, but I was utterly powerless. It was as though someone had started playing really explicit sex scenes on the projector. But way, way worse. Because it was actually sexy and featured you. That was a rough day."

"I'm sorry."

"Are you?"

I laugh. "I'm not sure. Undecided."

His face softens. "You know, some of my favourite daydreams of yours are the ones where you're just imagining us having a really tender moment. The daydreams where I'm stroking your hair and kissing you. I'm sure I remember one where I was bringing you chocolate and a hot-water bottle."

That's somehow more embarrassing than the kinky thoughts. "Must have been on my period," I quip, trying to act nonchalant even though I'm now curled up in his arms and he's gently stroking my hair. I can literally feel the oxytocin flooding my entire body, the dopamine pinging around my brain.

"I know, for example, that you like having your hair stroked," he says, his voice all low and inviting.

"Maybe it's not all bad, this gift."

"Maybe, but this is probably the only time in my life that I recall it being an advantage." He's trying to be funny, but I can see the sadness in his expression.

"Tom, what did you think when you first came up here and saw me?"

I've been wanting to know ever since he saw me but, for obvious reasons, it didn't seem appropriate to bring it up before now.

"I thought you were a mirage, all naked and beautiful, lying there in the starlight like that. I thought I'd gone mad. It was only when you saw me and panicked that I realised you weren't."

"So you watched?"

He looks troubled. "Emilie, I genuinely thought you were a magical apparition. I didn't stop to think why or how. I was completely taken in by the sight of you. I would never have carried on watching had I known. Honestly, you were the last person I was expecting to find up here."

"And before you realised I wasn't an apparition, what did you think?"

He frowns. "I've never been gut-punched by desire like that before. Guess there's a first time for everything…"

I can't decide if I'm flattered, or embarrassed, or both.

"Did the slippers not distract from the overall experience?"

"I can assure you, they most certainly did not."

His reply is so hilariously sincere that I try to stifle a laugh and it turns into a snort. Attractive. This, in turn, cracks him up. We're both helpless for several minutes. Finally, after the laughter starts to subside, he gets up to pour another drink.

"Can you see dreams?" I ask him.

He nods. "I can," he says, returning to the sofa. I'm immediately grateful that he's back, his body pressed to my side, his arm around me. "Dreams are an odd one. They're not nearly as ordered as we try to make them after we wake up. They're mostly random and nonsensical and messy. Not very interesting to watch. Not unless someone's having a night terror."

I'm really trying to imagine what it must be like to see dreams. Do they fill the room like my fantasies do? Does he see them or just hear them?

Of course, he answers my question before I vocalise it. "I see dreams just above people's heads," he tells me. "Sometimes they're little short video clips in quick succession. Sometimes it's like looking at a series of fast-moving images, as though someone's flipping through photos really quickly. But the images, some of them, are abstract. Or they look normal at first, until I realise something's off. Like, the image is of someone walking a dog in the park. But the dog has triangle eyes and is floating in the air like a kite."

"Wow, that sounds trippy."

"And dreams are very rarely three-dimensional in the way your daydreams are. But, on the rare occasion the dreams *are* vivid enough to be three-dimensional, you can guarantee that the dream is actually a nightmare. I walked into my bedroom once and Frederic – my roommate – was having a night terror. Scared the shit out of me when I saw the menacing, shadowy figure in the corner of the room. I yelped in surprise, which woke Frederic up. I had to pretend I'd stubbed my toe on the bed."

I shake my head. This stuff is mad, absolutely mad. I had no idea. And I have so many more questions. What does he know that he shouldn't? When did he realise he wasn't normal? Did his parents ever find out?

I feel him pull away from me, and I have to stop myself from dragging him back like some needy kraken.

"We've been up here a long time," he says. "We should go to bed."

I groan.

Quietly, so quietly that I struggle to hear him, he says, "We could meet tomorrow night."

I look at him. He's turned away from me, unable to meet my eye. He's still so conflicted about this, and I understand; it's a huge risk.

"It'll be harder to get away tomorrow night," I muse aloud. "Everyone stays up late on a Saturday night – it's party night." And I'm usually an active, enthusiastic participant, even if I'm only able to get high on sugar. "So if I disappear, it'll be noticed."

He nods slowly. "Okay."

"But I'm sure I can get away. It'll have to be a bit later. After midnight. How about one?"

He nods again. "That could work."

I don't want him to go; don't want this to end. So, like a child, I steer the conversation back to my favourite subject.

"You know all my fantasies," I say. "I want to know yours."

He smiles. He knows what I'm doing. "Maybe."

"Why only 'maybe'?"

He immediately looks sombre. "I'm being so irresponsible. A clandestine affair with a pupil. If I get fired and reported for gross misconduct, it'll be no less than I deserve."

"I'm a student, not a pupil. I'm not a minor. Old enough to vote, drink, drive a car…" I'm trying to reassure him, but I can tell I'm losing the battle.

He gets to his feet. He looks sad.

"Tomorrow night?" I ask, trying to keep the desperation from my voice.

When he replies, his voice cracks.

"Tomorrow night, then," he says.

5

I don't see him all of Saturday. I don't usually see him on the weekends, so this is no surprise, but my anxiety grows the longer we're apart. I'm nervous. Given his sombre mood when he left in the early hours, I can't be certain he'll show.

In the morning, when I get woken by my roommates, I have my excuse prepared and I'm able to shower in peace while everyone is out at the cinema. I make a mental note to power through my next period so no one twigs I've lied.

I'm so preoccupied the entire day; his face, his dazzling smile, burnt into my retina. That evening, when everyone's sharing Skittles and stories about underwhelming boys, I smile serenely, hoping everyone buys into my period excuse. I feel like I'm living in a bubble, counting the hours.

Instead of listening to Sara relay the complex rules of a card game we're supposed to be playing, I'm thinking about what I'm going to wear. Do I dare wear my skimpiest, laciest pyjamas? Or is that an assumption? I already know this isn't some mindless fling, a shallow relationship that's only about the sex. He knows my most intimate thoughts; knows me better than is entirely comfortable. I decide on the pretty, sheer pyjama set, but I'll wear my boring, school-issue black wool cloak over the top. It's an odd contradiction; I'm just another pupil (student!) here, following convention. But I'm also older, different. Independent, mature, a woman.

By the time I climb those stairs, my stomach's a churning, swooping mess of mixed feelings. Yesterday, this didn't feel so complicated. Tonight, as I scale the steps, my palms damp, I wonder what on earth I'm thinking. His doubts, the ones he was so evidently being eaten by yesterday, have been haunting me today.

When I reach the top of the stairs, the observatory is empty. It's later than we'd arranged to meet, and I'm convinced he won't come, that last night was the start and end of our romantic entanglement. To distract myself, I begin searching cupboards, looking for the rum and the glass that were here yesterday. Despite my searching, I can't find them, and I don't know why, but it makes my heart hurt.

I sit on the sofa, look out at the horizon and wrap my cloak tighter around myself. I'm not wearing a watch, so I don't know exactly how many minutes past one it is. I only know that when I left my room, it was gone ten past, my roommates starting to doze on their beds. I had to wait until Sara, still riding her sugar high, had gone to the bathroom before making my escape. I hope she isn't wondering where I am.

I think about the burden of his secrets. I imagine what it must be like, to live with such a huge power, one you don't want. The rest of us, we get to choose, to learn the magic we want for ourselves. Tom, with his rare power – a power he was born with – doesn't have that choice.

I close my eyes; let my head rest on the back of the sofa. I can't shake the sorrow that has come to rest, like the ghost of a dead bird, on my chest.

I wait, and my mind, as it often does, drifts. I think about the way magic is portrayed in film, how real magic is so much harder; I can barely light a candle, let alone do some of the incredibly powerful magic kids do in movies. In real life, not everyone learns magic, just those who are open-minded enough to believe in it. The only difference between me and someone who doesn't do magic is self-belief. It's a bit like *The Matrix* in that way, where Neo doesn't make the jump to the neighbouring skyscraper because he doesn't believe enough.

I'm wide awake when I hear someone climb the last few steps. I know it's him. When I turn to look, I notice he's holding a bottle of something in one hand, two glasses in the other. My heart soars.

"I'm sorry I'm late. Frederic split up with his girlfriend and needed company. I got away as soon as I could." He's slightly out of breath.

It occurs to me that he can read my unadulterated delight; see the fireworks in my brain. Playing it cool, distant, isn't an option for me, and I find myself laughing. I'm so relieved.

He puts the bottle and two crystal glasses on the countertop and, finally, looks at me. I'm no telepath, but I can tell he's happy to see me.

"You were worried I wasn't coming," he says.

"You seemed so... anxious, last time," I explain. "I wasn't certain."

He pours two glasses and hands me one, then sits beside me on the sofa, only a few inches away. There's a confidence to him this time. I wonder where it stems from – what's changed.

I take a sip. It's the same delicious, sweet-salty golden rum from last time. Bliss. I wonder where he bought it.

"There's a shop in town. Local distillery. Small batch, hand-crafted."

"Impressive."

He holds up the crystal glass to me, expectant. I chink mine against his, the sound ringing like anticipation out into the quiet, still air.

Neither of us say a word. To say anything would be pre-emptive, presumptive. I take another sip.

"What did you do today?" I ask eventually.

"I had to be umpire – for a cricket match – at the all-boys school. I regretted volunteering for that when I crawled out of bed at half six this morning, let me tell you." He chuckles quietly to himself. "You might as well have been there, sat on the grass in front of me, deep in your vivid daydreams. I couldn't think of anything else. I was a hopeless umpire. I hope no one noticed."

I am, naturally, delighted.

"I see..." I say, trying to play it cool. He can, of course, see right through it, but I'm at least trying. I so badly want to reach out and touch him. But I don't; I force myself to wait.

"How was your day?" he asks. He relaxes into the sofa, his free arm resting along the back of it, his fingers just inches from my shoulders.

"I managed a lie-in. And a shower in peace while everyone else was out at the cinema."

He groans, smiles, looks out of the window. "I'm jealous."

"I bet," I tease. "I'm lucky no one's keeping track of my menstrual cycle. My white lie was so convincing that one of the girls brought me a share-sized bar of chocolate. I felt terrible for at least a minute."

He chuckles; a warm, inviting sound that emanates from his chest.

"Sounds like my day was easier than yours," I say. "You managed to console Frederic?"

"I think so. His girlfriend dumped him yesterday. He seemed okay when I left."

There's a pause while he takes a sip of his drink. Something is definitely different.

"What do you want, Emilie?" he asks. His eyes are on mine, his gaze unwavering. His new confidence is unnerving. I swallow.

The truth is, I want whatever I can get, even if it means nursing a broken heart for years to come. But I don't want to say that because it seems desperate.

Of course, it's too late.

"But if you could *choose*?" he asks, reading my mind. "If you could have whatever you wanted?"

I think I understand his question. Am I looking for some incredibly high risk, self-indulgent fling or something more meaningful?

"The latter," I say, hoping he understands. I'm scared to follow this train of thought, knowing he can literally read my mind. I don't want to spend a second longer analysing my feelings for him. Later, maybe. In private. I've known this man for two years, spending several hours a week in his company but conducting my relationship with him almost entirely in my head.

"What do *you* want?" I bat back. I think I know, but I want confirmation.

He shakes his head, seeming irritated. "I'd have thought that was obvious. If I was looking for no-strings sex, I could find something considerably less complicated elsewhere."

Stupid question. Of course he could. My cheeks grow warm.

"Sorry, that was unfair," he says immediately. He puts his glass down and takes my free hand, sandwiching it between both of his. "I want you so badly. And I'm terrified. It's making me short. I'm sorry."

I dare to look at him again. "We could wait," I suggest, even though it's not what I want at all. "We could wait until the summer when I'll no longer technically be a student here."

He says nothing initially, but his pained expression has returned. "That would make the most sense," he says, but he doesn't sound convinced. At all.

I relax my grip and allow my cloak to fall open enough that he can see my bare leg and a tiny bit of lace on my pyjama shorts.

He exhales as though someone is wringing the breath out of him. "But I don't want to wait," he gasps. "I've waited for longer than you probably realise. I tried to blot you out when I first saw you, but it was impossible. You're beautiful, Emilie, pure gold; you're the moon and the stars and the sun. Do you know that? Do you know how utterly captivating you are?"

He's now kneeling before me, as though he's worshipping me. His hands are gently massaging my calves.

"And the way you always wear your hair up. A plaited halo of spun gold. Yesterday, when I saw what I thought was a mirage of you, I thought maybe my time had come, that it was the end. And what a sweet ending it would have been."

His fingers are caressing the soft, sensitive skin behind my knees now. I'm wet already.

"I want to give you exactly what you want," he says, his voice nearly a whisper.

I part my legs, letting the cloak fall completely open. He groans then shuts his eyes like it's all too much. I glance down at myself to see what he sees, noticing the way my breasts look, my hard nipples visible through the fine, silky fabric.

He opens his eyes again, this time allowing himself to look at me. "Good God," he says simply, visibly choked.

I've never felt more beautiful or turned on in my life. I want everything, all at once, like a greedy child at an ice cream parlour. I want him to bite my nipples; I want him to part my legs and fill me up. I want to suck him, have him come in my mouth, hear him cry out.

His eyes are wide with wonder. I shuffle towards the edge of the sofa so I'm closer to him, and he takes my face in his hands. His pupils are huge and black, and I feel my stomach swoop as though I'm on a rollercoaster. He's going to kiss me.

We both see it at the same time – a change in the light; the shadow on the wall flickers. His face is frozen in a look of pure terror. We wait, our breath held, to see what follows. Nothing. It was nothing. My brain takes a couple of seconds to register what we saw: almost certainly just a bat, flying past the window.

We both sag with relief, but I can't forget the expression on his face. What in the actual fuck are we doing? He was right – there's simply too much at stake.

He doesn't need to be able to read my mind to know what I'm thinking.

"*Emilie*," he pleads.

And suddenly I understand the source of his newfound confidence: he's already made up his mind. He's prepared to take the risk, to put his career on the line, for me. He's okay with that. But I'm not. While my humiliation would be temporary, the cost to him would be lifelong.

I leap up.

"Emilie!"

6

I'M ON EDGE ALL of Sunday, hyped up on caffeine because I'm drinking tea as a substitute for food. My appetite is non-existent; I feel as though I've swallowed a boulder.

The girls are concerned about me and my lack of appetite; thank God I can lean on my period excuse. "Day two," I mumble at them. They understand. I receive at least three sympathetic shoulder squeezes, and one of them loans me her favourite, dog-eared paperback to take my mind off it. But not even tales of Becky's singed eyebrows – the girl will insist on dicking about with fire magic – can distract me. The guilt is awful; I hate lying. I have to swallow my self-loathing. It tastes bitter.

I'm confident I won't see him today, but I have a lesson with him tomorrow, Monday, last thing. Every time I think of it, my stomach clenches and I feel nauseated. I'm conflicted: I could pull a sickie for that lesson, but there's a risk I'll get sent to see the nurse for an interrogation, and I'm not sure how much longer I can fake it. If I avoid looking at him, if I concentrate solely on the work, I might be able to get through those fifty minutes.

It's only as I file into the great hall for assembly on Monday that I remember: Tom is leaving, and it'll be announced today. Imminently. Which means he'll be here. How had I forgotten? Dissociative amnesia, perhaps? And in that second, I glance up, and our eyes meet. Shit. I look away immediately, but I'm trembling. Can he hear my thoughts from this distance away? I wonder. Surely they'll be drowned out by everyone else's? I should have quizzed him more when I had the opportunity.

For the most part, it's the usual assembly – the head gives his spiel about community values and spellcasting safety, we sing some songs and Mr Saddler tries not to nod off. But with five minutes of assembly remaining, the head beckons Tom to the front after telling us he'll be leaving. Feeling safe, tucked away in the crowd, I allow myself the luxury (or torment, I can't decide which) of studying him. He's wearing his usual teacher attire – crisp shirt, well-fitting trousers, thin black tie, nice shoes. I can feel my body responding to him – an ache in my chest, my heart beating between my legs. It's ridiculous. I try, and fail, to avoid thinking about the events of Friday night. Then, like a laser, his eyes are on me. Shit. I hope he hasn't "heard" me.

He gives a short, platitude-laden speech. He's loved working here, been grateful for the opportunity, has learnt so much, will miss us, etcetera. I swear I see at least five girls tear up. It's no surprise; I'm not the only one who has a crush on him.

Then assembly is over, thank God. But the afternoon rolls on, and before I know it, it's 4 p.m. and I'm due in class with him.

I steel myself as I enter. Avoiding eye contact like the plague, I sit at the back of the classroom, earning me strange looks from the group I usually sit with. I pull a sad face, to imply that I'm sitting at the back because I feel unwell. I'm not sure they understand me.

I try and focus on the lesson, but it's a full-time job to keep my thoughts in check. It strikes me how accustomed my brain is to fantasising about him whenever he's nearby. Time for some serious mental reprogramming, methinks.

At long last, the lesson is nearly over. I'm packed up and nearly out of my seat when he speaks.

"Emilie, will you stay behind? I need a word."

Fuck.

As everyone files out, it strikes me that this is unnecessarily risky. The door clicks shut behind us.

"Are you mad?" I hiss at him.

"What choice do I have?" he hisses back. "You've made this nigh-on impossible."

"Yes. Intentionally."

"Please, will you just hear me out?" he says, exasperated.

I pull a face but say nothing.

He draws up a chair and sits beside me as though he's explaining some tricky concept I need help with. With the subtlest of hand movements, he closes the blinds and quietly locks the door.

Then he carefully takes hold of my arm. Turning my palm to the sky, he starts stroking the inside of my wrist with his fingers. I have to look away.

"Emilie," he says quietly. His voice is soft and warm and low.

I swallow, then turn back to face him.

"I wouldn't be nearly this pushy if I thought you didn't want me," he continues. "But I know you're keeping your distance because you're worried for me. That's my decision, my risk to take. I can't stress that enough."

He's adamant. I can feel my resolve crumbling in the face of his determination. He has a point – I can't control him or live his life for him – but he's also not playing fair.

"You're taking advantage," I say.

He snatches his hand away as if my arm was red-hot steel.

"If you couldn't read my mind, we wouldn't be having this conversation."

He hesitates. He knows I'm right.

"Okay," he says simply.

My heart squeezes as he turns to look away, hurt written all over his face. We're silent for several moments.

"I guess this really is it, then."

I feel like I've been shot. The sensation is physical. My eyes well up, and I struggle to swallow the lump that's appeared in my throat. He doesn't move or say a word.

The tick-tock of the school-issue clock fills the classroom, and neither of us move for at least a minute.

Finally, I crack. I can't take it anymore. "Are you absolutely sure?" I whisper, choking back tears. The question is ambiguous, but I don't need to clarify. He knows exactly what I mean.

"I'm absolutely certain," he says, a dogged expression on his face that I've never seen before.

Tears stream down my face as though someone's turned on a tap.

He takes my face in his hands. "Let me show you."

I think he's going to kiss me, but instead he wipes my tears with his thumbs and then stands, pulling me to my feet.

"Over here," he says. He leads me to the front of the class, and I twig where he's taking me. We stand beside the desk that featured in my rudest of fantasies.

"Lie over the desk, Emilie," he says, his voice husky and low.

I carefully lower myself onto the desk until my breasts and stomach press against the wood. I part my legs. I want this so much it's left me mute.

"Good girl," he says, then slides his hands beneath my skirt and pulls my knickers off in one quick movement. I whimper and arch my back.

"Patience," he says, caressing my newly naked behind. But I hear his tell-tale ragged exhale; he's struggling just as much as I am.

My socks are knee high, and my skirt is up around my waist. Only my thighs and bottom are exposed. His hand feels warm on my cool skin. He cups my bare cheek and groans, then whips his hand away.

"Wait."

He's doing something – I hear the sound of fabric-on-fabric – and when he appears next to me, I see he's holding a black silk tie. I hold my wrists together in anticipation, my breathing laboured.

"I'm not going to blindfold you today," he says casually, letting me know this won't be the first and only time we do this. I squirm in anticipatory pleasure, wishing the desk were a few inches longer. I'm so very ready.

"Next time might involve a riding crop," he states, matter-of-fact.

I part my legs wider. "Please, sir," I huff. He's been paying close attention to my fantasies if he's remembered that detail.

I gasp as I hear his belt clatter to the floor. It's impossible to articulate just how much I want this. My brain is mush. I've been reduced to a trembling, wet, horny mass of desire.

"I'll be gentle," he says quietly, knowing that's exactly how I like it.

He eases the tip into me, and I cry out.

"Shhhh, Emilie," he whispers.

This is madness; we're taking such an unbelievable risk, but this only serves to turn me on further.

"More," I plead, tilting my hips up towards him.

"Patience," he pants in the sternest voice he can manage. I hear him break character and curse under his breath.

He gently eases more of himself into me so he's about halfway in. The sensation of being filled, of my ache being so tenderly met, is indescribably exquisite. He reaches up and takes hold of my plait, pulling it very gently as he eases the rest of his cock inside me. I think I might die.

An inelegant grunt is all I can manage. If I had my eyes open, they'd be crossed with pleasure. I'm on the very brink.

He's stock-still, pressed deeply into me. His other hand reaches down and brushes the sensitive skin of my inner thigh.

"You're so wet," he whispers, all pretence broken, no longer necessary.

I grunt again in reply. In my bliss-addled brain, three words float to the forefront of my consciousness: *I love this.* Every cell in my body has been crying out for it.

"Me too, Emilie," he whispers. "So very much."

His fingers reach the apex and begin to circle. I'm done for.

Wave after wave after wave crashes over me. I see colours, fireworks, sound. I squeeze the desk as hard as I can to stop myself from making too much noise.

When I'm finally done, a quivering mess slumped over a classroom desk, I feel him carefully withdraw.

I somehow hoist myself up onto my elbows and twist to face him. "What are you doing?" I protest. I'm determined to make this man come.

He laughs softly. "At some point, we need to have a conversation about contraception."

I say nothing, a plan forming. I present my wrists to him so he'll untie me, which he duly does. I try not to stare at his enormous erection, jutting proudly from beneath his white shirt. His black boxers and trousers are still around his ankles.

Before he has a chance to dress himself, I take hold of his cock.

"Emilie—"

"Shhh!" I tell him. My turn to be stern. I begin to stroke him, paying special attention to the tip.

"Wait!"

He grabs my wrist, but it's too late. He comes; great creamy spurts geyser forth like a hot spring. His face is contorted, a mixture of intense pleasure and surprise. It is absolutely glorious.

His cock throbs in my hand, and eventually the throbs subside. He's breathing heavily, a hand now resting on my shoulder to keep himself upright.

"My God," he utters.

I glance down at my skirt, my naked thighs, the floor. Shit.

I look up at him guiltily. His expression matches mine. A shy grin creeps onto his face.

"Looks like we've got some cleaning up to do," he says.

7

We dress ourselves in a hurry and clean up. We check and double-check, paranoid. I'm desperate for post-coitus affection, but I know we're taking a huge risk just by being here. It's approaching 6 p.m., long after classes have usually finished, so anyone seeing us now would have cause to wonder. We can't afford to loiter.

"Observatory later?" he asks when we're finally satisfied there's no evidence of our tryst remaining.

"Yes. Midnight?"

He nods. A twitch of his hand, and I hear the door unlock. "As we leave together, I'm going to make conversation as though I've had to work late to help you with a problem, okay?"

I nod dumbly. I'm glad someone is thinking about this stuff.

He opens the door; motions for me to step through it.

"Does that make sense now, then?" he says.

I play along. "Yes it does, thank you. I appreciate you taking the time to explain it."

"Any time, Emilie. I'm always happy to. You never need worry about asking."

He locks the door and tests the handle. I surreptitiously scan the corridors to check we're alone. We are, thank God.

"Catch you later," he says cheerily, in his usual teacher voice.

When I return to my dorm, Sara notices me immediately.

"Wow, you're looking better."

"Yeah, I feel it."

"Where were you?"

"Just with Mr Wakefield." No better lie than the truth.

She laughs. "Oh, that explains it then!" She's only joking, but the interaction makes my palms sweat. "God, he's hot, isn't he?"

"Yup. It was really no hardship to have him explain quantum field theory to me for an hour, let me tell you."

"I'm gutted he's leaving."

"Urgh, me too. Who will we lust over now? It's a travesty."

I entertain myself for the rest of the evening with the battered paperback that was kindly loaned to me by one of the other girls. Luckily, it's a Monday night so everyone is sound asleep by 11 p.m. I'm absolutely wired, as though I've been chugging caffeine despite having nothing of the sort. At 11.50 p.m., I slip out of bed and make my way to the observatory.

He's already there, lighting candles as I arrive. He greets me with a look of unbridled happiness.

He motions to the sofa, and I inch towards it.

"It's actually a futon," he says, fumbling beneath the teal velvet throw. A moment later, the sofa is flat like a bed.

"Ha! I never knew that." I'm surprised when he immediately reverts it.

"We can't be too careful," he says in response to my quizzical expression. Then he kicks off his shoes and climbs onto it, beckoning me to do the same. The warm, affectionate look he gives me makes my insides melt and my heart feel like a helium-filled balloon.

"Oh, Emilie," he sighs as I slide on beside him. He pulls me close so we're pressed tightly together, and my brain turns to scrambled egg. I've probably imagined something similar to this a thousand times, but I never in a million years thought it would happen.

"What made up your mind?" I ask. "You seem so certain."

Somehow, he pulls me closer. "I can move countries, switch careers, get a different job, but I might never find someone like you again in my entire life. *That's* the risk I can't take, Emilie."

My mind is blown. I've never been so... wanted. So adored. It's intoxicating. I sneak a look at his face, and my heart nearly stops. I can't believe this man is mine. His eyes are the colour of dark chocolate with a beautiful amber halo around the pupil. How have I never noticed this before? The answer is immediately obvious: we've never been this close before. I arrange myself so I can study his face better. His expression is a mixture of amusement and delight. I can't believe this is my life now. I fight with myself, trying not to laugh at the ridiculousness of it. A smile plays on his lips, too.

Suddenly, his expression changes and I feel his whole body stiffen. "Oh God. That wasn't your first time, was it?"

I can't help but laugh. "No. Although I wish it had been."

He shakes his head. "I should have thought to ask about that before now. Christ. I'm sorry."

"You don't need to apologise."

"Well, I don't know about that; I should have offered you a drink by now," he says before standing up and walking over to the worktop, his socked feet silent on the stone floor.

When he returns, two drinks in hand, he sits on the edge of the futon. I can't decide whether to sit on his lap or not. I settle for sitting next to him, one of my legs draped diagonally across his. After handing me my drink, he rests his free hand on my bare knee, cupping it.

"I'll never be able to drink this without thinking of you now," he says, chinking his glass against mine.

I can't help but smile at that.

I inhale the delicious aroma, close my eyes and take a sip.

"So good," I murmur. And for a short time I'm quiet, completely in the moment, lapping up every detail – the intense salty tang of the rum, the warmth of Tom's body beside me, the smell of a distant bonfire. My mindfulness teacher would be proud.

"I can't wait to take you out," he says from beside me. His voice is low, shy, but I can sense a childlike excitement behind it. Mentally, I think, he's further ahead than me. This is all so sudden I've barely considered how we'll conceal our relationship for the next week. But now that I think of it, dating is a thrilling concept. I turn to face him.

"I have a restaurant in mind for our first date," he continues. "I think you'll absolutely love it."

And, I think, he'll get to see me in something other than this drab, school-issue cloak. Black never was my colour. Despite the undercurrent of unease, the risks I'm all too aware we're taking, it's hard not to feel excited.

My thoughts turn to the fact that I won't be here, at this school, for much longer. I haven't decided exactly where I'm going to uni yet, only that I will. What will happen then?

"We'll figure it out," he assures me. "I'll move again if I need to. In fact, the further away from here we are, the better. You were considering Scotland, were you not? Edinburgh?"

I nod, trying to suppress my next thought, but it won't be deterred: what if this relationship doesn't work out? He'll have sacrificed so much, and for what? Will he be left angry and resentful for having made such sacrifices?

"Never," he assures me. "But I might resent myself for never having given us a chance."

The intensity of his gaze pierces my heart, which is now leaping about wildly in my chest.

I take another sip of rum. His eyes remain resolutely on mine. Gently, he lifts the glass from my fingers and takes my wrists, pulling me on top of him so my full weight is pressing against him. His pupils are huge black holes, broadcasting his desire. I shift slightly, paranoid that I'm crushing him, and feel the blunt, solid length of his arousal against my stomach. I imagine how good it would feel to sit on it.

"Please," he whispers, a half groan. His expression is one of desperation.

It's not a warm room, so it's not practical for us both to strip naked. Instead, I unbutton the top three buttons of his shirt and kiss the skin just below the hollow dip of his throat. He sighs and moves beneath me.

We both hear it at the same time and freeze. Footsteps on the stairs; the sound is unmistakable. Someone is coming.

"Shit!" I hiss.

He says nothing, just points to a dark corner, a cabinet I can hide behind, and I make a dash for it. The last thing I see before I crouch behind the furniture is Tom nudging my shoes under the futon.

"Good evening!" It's Tom's voice. He sounds cheery, amiable.

As soon as I hear the other voice, I know who it is. "Ah. Good evening, Tom." The caretaker. I can see him clearly in my mind's eye: bad teeth, a lazy eye and a comb-over that does absolutely nothing to disguise his bald patch. "I wasn't expecting to find you up here," he says evenly.

"I came up here to watch the stars and have a drink in peace."

I suddenly remember: there were two glasses. Did Tom remember to hide mine? Panic spirals in my chest like a frightened flock of birds.

The caretaker grunts in response, something close to an agreement. "Peace isn't exactly easy to come by round here."

"Quite."

"Well, as it's you and not some reprobate students, I can overlook it." I hear a shuffle, and I hope that means he's leaving. "Rather romantic up here, isn't it?"

I feel sick. Could he somehow know about us? Fear squeezes my lungs, and it's an effort to keep my breathing quiet.

I hear Tom make a small noise, a half-laugh. Non-committal. Wise, I think. Protest too much and it looks suspicious.

"Good evening, Tom," the caretaker says.

"You too."

Even after the footsteps have faded, I wait behind the cabinet until Tom coaxes me out.

"Fuck," I say. I look around. Tom did remember to hide the second glass after all, thank all that's holy. But the caretaker was right; it's a romantic setting, especially with the soft light provided by the candles. Despite the cold, I realise I'm actually sweating. Tom has yet to speak.

I look at him. His forehead is creased with worry.

"We won't get any peace while we're on school grounds," he says eventually. He looks crushed. "He was suspicious."

"You heard his thoughts?"

"Yes. Bastard doesn't miss a trick."

"Fuck." I perch on the edge of the futon, defeated. "What did you hear?"

"Nothing specific, but I detected his doubt. He probably thinks I'm having an affair with one of the teachers."

I let it sink in, yet again: the enormity of what we're doing, the risks we're taking.

"Let's go away for the weekend," he says suddenly, and I can tell from his tone that he's determined. Our terrifyingly close call with the caretaker has done nothing to deter him.

"We could…" I say, letting my mind mull this concept over, already plotting how I'd explain my absence. My parents are three hours away by train, a reasonable distance for a weekend visit, and a perfectly reasonable explanation for my whereabouts. "Where would we go?" I ask. "Kielder Forest Park?"

"We could, although it'll be muddier at this time of year. We're less than two hours from Scotland; we could go to the coast."

Yes! Scotland. I feel positively buoyant at the thought. I've always wanted to go, but despite its proximity I've never made it over the border.

I look at him; his eyes are shining with excitement.

"Yes," I say, fighting the urge to do an excited little jig. "Let's go to Scotland."

8

I'M EXHAUSTED ON TUESDAY, but it's that weird kind of exhaustion mixed with excitement that has me feeling light-headed and dizzy. I nearly fall asleep in Mrs Bender's class, but luckily Sara nudges me awake before anyone notices.

I can't stop thinking about Scotland. Last night, Tom and I discussed logistics. On Saturday, I'll meet him mid-morning at the train station on the outskirts of town. From there, we'll drive up to Scotland – just two hours away – together. I have no idea where we'll be staying or exactly what we'll see while we're there. He practically begged me to leave all that to him. I smile every time I recall his excitement and desire to surprise me.

What we didn't discuss last night was whether we'd see each other before the weekend. I realise now that this was a huge oversight. Saturday feels several centuries away.

"You okay?"

It's Sara. We're in the common room, vegging between classes. She must have caught me smiling.

I shake myself. "Sorry. Yeah. Fine."

"You've been in the weirdest mood today. Exhausted but smiley. You haven't taken a lover, have you?"

I actually spit out my tea, spraying liquid from my mouth like a garden hose. Sara collapses into hysterical laughter.

"I can't believe you just did that!" she says, tears quite literally running down the sides of her face.

"Neither can I," I say, looking in dismay at the mess I've made. I spot the paper towels on the counter and walk over to get them. As I start to mop up the tea, I decide to use humour to throw her off the scent.

"A lover would be a fine thing for a heterosexual woman like me in a school full of other women."

Sara is still wiping tears from her eyes. "True. There's a distinct lack of dick around here."

I shouldn't laugh at that, but I do. "Tell me about it."

I can't escape the feeling I've narrowly avoided something. I finish mopping up the tea and return to my chair.

"Oh, by the way, I'm going home at the weekend," I tell her. The lie slips out so easily it's frankly disturbing. "I might pop into town before I go – try and find something half-decent to wear. Something that isn't school-issue and black. Wanna come with?"

It occurs to me, as I offer this, that I'll almost certainly want to buy lingerie, too. Oh well. Guess I'll somehow negotiate that while we're out. Sara's eye for fashion and insightful feedback on my outfits are far too valuable to miss out on.

Her eyes light up. "Yes! Count me in!"

Sara loves shopping. And dressing me. It's a shame her parents are insisting she study medicine so she can use her magic to heal people; she'd make a great personal stylist.

"Tomorrow afternoon?"

"Sure!"

We usually get Wednesday afternoons off unless there's some special event scheduled. Those that don't have sports matches to attend often venture into town to escape the campus for a bit.

Just as we're finishing our drinks, the bell rings, signalling the end of our free period and the start of the last lesson of the day.

"Time for our all-too-meagre dose of hot man," Sara jests. "Try not to stare at his crotch the entire time, hey?"

"I make no promises," I joke.

Christ, if only she knew.

As soon as I walk in, I see the enormous cup of coffee on Tom's desk and have to contain my laughter. As I make my way to my usual seat, he glances at me for a split second, and our eyes meet. His poker face is perfect. My stomach somersaults. I hope I've managed to keep my face neutral, too.

I'm kicking myself for not having thought to arrange our next meeting, but perhaps this was intentional on Tom's part; the more we meet in person, the greater the risk we'll get caught. One could argue that the weekend will be all the sweeter for the wait, but I'm pretty sure I won't make it to Saturday if I don't see him before then. Spontaneous combustion is a rare phenomenon, but I'm sure I read somewhere that it can be caused by intense sexual longing.

I settle in my seat, and my eyes drift to the empty desk at the front of the class. Thank God furniture can't talk.

I turn my attention to the board. We're studying wave theory and levitation at the moment. For Tom's sake and my own, I make myself a promise: today, I will concentrate exclusively on the material. And this works, sort of. During our lesson, I'm able to avoid looking at him, which helps, but truthfully it's much tougher than I anticipated. With just five minutes left of the lesson, it seems my willpower has evaporated. I simply can't hold back the thoughts that are there waiting for me.

I imagine I'm on my knees, my back against the classroom wall. Tom is pinning both of my hands above my head. His fly is unzipped, his cock is in my mouth, and he's carefully easing more of himself into me. I'm groaning, wet, greedily sucking, desperate to taste him. He's panting, eyes tightly closed, desperately trying not to come. There's nothing hotter than the thought of him having to fight for self-control.

I imagine my shirt is unbuttoned halfway, my bra-free breasts nearly completely visible, the rough cotton brushing against my nipples.

I'm desperate to have him come in my mouth, but instead he pulls out, ejaculating all over my throat and chin, the thick white fluid dribbling down onto my breasts and soaking my shirt. Under the table, I shift in my seat.

In my periphery, I see him hesitate for just a moment. It's such a small movement that I can't imagine anyone else would have noticed. I see him reach for his coffee, his knuckles white around his ceramic travel cup, and immediately I feel awful. I'm officially A Terrible Person. I put my head in my hands, unable to look at him, and will my mind to go blank.

A few minutes later, when I look up, Tom is handing out exercise books having marked our last assignments. My book is already on my desk, and I open it, curious about my grade, to find a folded Post-it nestled between the pages. Making sure no one else can see it, I prise the note open with my fingers.

"*Meet me in SB.1,*" it says.

9

It's already starting to get dark outside. Classroom SB.1 is in one of the more remote teaching spaces, away from the bulk of the buildings that make up the main campus. I make my excuses to Sara after our lesson and take the poorly lit route, moving swiftly through the shadows like a fully-fledged ninja.

He's already there when I arrive, standing at the front of the class as if ready to teach, and the look on his face gives nothing away.

"Take a seat," he says, motioning to the desks before he closes the blinds and locks the door. It's only once I've sat down I notice he's rearranged some of the desks.

"I think we need to discuss… your behaviour," he says, pursing his lips, his tone impassive. His expression is carefully neutral, and for a split second I wonder if he's serious. What a hilarious disaster it would be if I'd misunderstood – if I were really here to be disciplined for my behaviour.

"Your focus in my lessons has been... lacking. Abysmal, really, if I'm being honest with you, Emilie."

I nod, biting down on my lower lip to prevent a smile from forming. "I'm sorry."

"I'm sorry, *sir*," he corrects. Which is hilarious because he never insists anyone calls him sir. Everyone calls him Mr Wakefield, even in sixth form. And that's how I know what I'm here for.

"I'm sorry, *sir*," I repeat.

"Better."

His face softens slightly, his expression brooding. I shift in my seat, feeling the blood rush between my legs. I want him – this – so much.

"I hope you'll understand that this kind of behaviour cannot go unpunished." He sighs, faux resigned. He tries to look apologetic. "For such a sustained period of misbehaviour, there must be consequences."

I nod. "Yes, sir."

"Take off your knickers."

His expression is completely deadpan. I'm instantly wet.

I wiggle so I can remain seated while I complete my task, pulling my knickers off and stuffing them into my bag. I look at him, expectant.

"Good. Open your legs."

I do as I'm told. He walks towards the blackboard so that he can see beneath my desk. I watch his composure take a hit, his tiny tell-tale sigh an indication of his struggle. He turns; takes two steps towards me.

"Get on the floor. On all fours."

I rise from the desk, walk around to the front and comply. The floor is dusty beneath my palms and knees. But then he seems to disappear. From my position on the floor, I can't see past the front desk. He suddenly reappears, a brand-new-looking black riding crop in his hand. I release a shuddery sigh. *Oh*.

"I'm sorry, sir," I say, wondering how on *earth* he managed to smuggle a riding crop into a classroom.

"No, *I'm* sorry, Emilie. I'm sorry it's come to this," he replies. His enormous erection, jutting out from his trousers, is evidence to the contrary. He's not sorry at all, and neither am I. This is exactly what I want. His precise recollection of the details of my fantasies honestly makes me wonder if he makes notes after our classes together.

He uses the riding crop to lift my skirt and rest the material on my back, my bare bottom exposed to the cool evening air, then caresses my skin with the tip as he runs it over my backside. I recognise the scent of new leather.

When he flicks the crop so it comes into contact with my bare skin, I jump and let out a small noise in surprise. But all I feel is the mildest sting, and my skin tingles, and it's then I understand. Having never done this before with anyone, I wasn't sure if reality would live up to the fantasy. But now I get it.

He moves the leather tip to where my buttock meets my thigh, only centimetres from my entrance. I'm sopping wet and desperate to be touched, licked, sucked. I want him to taste me.

"No, Emilie," he says, but his voice is low and husky, and when I look at his face, his eyes are enormous saucers of desire.

"Sorry, sir."

"You should be."

He hits me again, just slightly harder this time. I feel the sting, the tingle. It feels so good. He inches the leather tip closer to my wet lips.

"I know you fantasise about being watched, Emilie," he says, his voice like velvet. Of course he knows, because he knows everything, but it doesn't stop my cheeks from turning red. This is foreplay, I realise. Not only do I get to live out my filthiest fantasies with this man, but each time he teases me with the promise of what's to come.

"I can't think of a single man who wouldn't want to watch you. But you're far too distractable and impulsive. And that's why you're here." He hits me again, inner thigh this time, with exactly the right amount of force. I feel the crop edges towards my clitoris and stop short so that it rests just a centimetre away. He hits me again – three times in quick succession – three little stings, the soft, tender skin on my inner thigh tingling.

Finally, *finally*, he flicks the leather gently against my clitoris, and I nearly come just from that contact alone. It feels so. Fucking. Good.

"Please," I beg, my voice ragged, desperate.

"No."

I hear him rest the crop on the desk. *Damn* it.

"That's quite enough," he says, breathless. "Get up."

I do as I'm told, brushing off my skirt and my dusty knees. My legs are shaking.

"Go over to that desk and lie over it. On your front."

I comply. He approaches me, and I can see he has something in his hand. It's a black blindfold. He covers my eyes, carefully tying it behind my head.

"Hold on to the desk and don't let go until I tell you to."

I cling to the edge of it, knuckles white, hard wood pressed against my stomach.

I feel something pleasantly cool and hard against my inner thigh then, and I wonder what on earth it is. Tom traces lines oh so gently over my skin with it, but I'm still none the wiser. Then, so very slowly, I feel him insert the tip of it inside me, about an inch or so.

I grip the edge of the desk tighter. "God," I huff. The coolness, the hardness... it just feels so good. I want more. I arch my back and open my legs wider.

"Don't," he warns. But I can tell from his tone that he doesn't mean it. He sounds like Tom, not the strict school-teacher persona he dons for my amusement and titillation.

He eases more of it inside me, another inch. It's not completely smooth; I can feel its delicious ridges. I whimper and then bite my tongue, worried that if I beg, he'll stop.

He pushes it in deeper then starts to move it in a circular motion, and I can feel it nudging against my G-spot. I can't help but moan – loudly. I'm so unbelievably close.

Then I feel his fingers gently circling my wet clitoris, and that's when it's all over for me. It's all I can do not to fall off the desk as Tom pushes whatever it is deeper still – which is exactly what I want at that precise moment as I orgasm. I grip the desk harder as intense waves of pleasure wash over me. I'm making too much noise – I know I am – but I can't stop.

Finally, my body's throbs become less intense, and I just lie there, panting, my limbs like jelly.

"Oh, Emilie," Tom says. There's such warmth in his voice.

I remain still for a moment, not really knowing what to do. I'm not sure my legs will support me if I try to get up.

"You can let go of the desk now," he says, his voice light and teasing.

I giggle. "Thank you, sir."

He takes off the blindfold, and I carefully stand, looking for whatever it was that was just inside me, but I can't see anything. When I turn to look at him, I see he's battling an enormous grin.

"Magic," he says, by way of explanation.

I point to the chair behind the desk. "Sit."

He smiles; shakes his head. "Emilie, we have to go. It's far too risky us being here, you know that. Another time."

"Sit," I command, my tone entirely non-negotiable this time. I mean it, and he knows it. Still, he hesitates. I put a hand on my hip and glare at him. His eyebrows shoot up, the corner of his mouth curls upwards and he makes his way over to the chair.

"Push it back so it's against the blackboard," I instruct. "Then sit."

He does, and before he can protest further, I'm on my knees, undoing his trousers and his boxers until his cock springs out, silky and hard. I begin to kiss it, and I hear his breathing change.

"Oh God," he moans.

I focus my attention on the tip, gently licking and kissing, as my hand starts to work the shaft. He leans back in the chair, finally admitting defeat.

I take my time; I don't want to rush. I slowly take him in my mouth and let his hips dictate the pace.

"Oh *fuck*," he says as he strokes my hair and caresses my face.

I take as much of him in my mouth as I possibly can. He grabs the arm of the chair and squirms in his seat.

"Ah! Oh!"

And then I taste it. Panting and moaning as I pin him to the chair, he comes – hard – in my mouth.

"Fuck!" he cries.

I wait. When I'm sure he's finally spent, I slowly withdraw and look up to admire the dreamy look on his face. His cheeks are red, his expression soft, a shy smile dancing on his face. I'm pretty sure my expression mirrors his. Then we both remember where we are.

"Um, I should..." he says, standing up slowly.

"Ah, yeah."

He starts to dress himself. I do the same. And the thought bounds, unbidden, into my head. What if someone saw us? Surely it's impossible, because the blinds are shut and the door is locked, and besides, it wouldn't be unusual for a teacher to be prepping in a classroom at this time of the evening. Still, I'm painfully aware of the risk we're taking. I remember the comment Sara made earlier.

He walks over to me. He looks worried, too.

"What's wrong?"

I sigh. "I think Sara's suspicious. I don't know, perhaps I'm just being paranoid. She made a joke in the common room earlier about me taking a lover. I can't tell if she was joking or whether she actually suspects something."

His face falls. "I think Frederic is starting to suspect something, too. He hasn't said anything to me, but he's noticed I'm tired a lot more than usual, and that I'm not in my room as much. The cogs are turning – I can hear them."

I put my face in my hands and groan. "I feel suffocated here," I say, my voice muffled. "It feels like everyone is watching us."

I want him to reassure me, to tell me I'm worrying unnecessarily, but he doesn't.

"We shouldn't meet again until the weekend. I don't want anything to compromise the Scotland trip."

I'm not thrilled about this, but he's absolutely right. "Okay," I concur. With only ten days until the Christmas break and Tom leaving, we'd be mad to take unnecessary risks now. And at the weekend, we'll have almost two whole days together in a town hours from here with the privacy and anonymity we both so badly need.

I look at him. I can tell he's tense.

"You leave first," he says. "I'll stay here – do some marking. No one will suspect anything out of the ordinary." He waves his hand, and I hear the door unlock.

I nod.

"See you on Saturday, Emilie," he says, walking back to his desk.

I turn to leave, feeling suddenly uneasy. But when I look back over my shoulder, he's looking at me with that warm, dreamy expression again, and I feel something bloom in my chest. Dear God, please let this all somehow be okay.

10

Sara has a gift for dressing people. I've never known anyone with such an eye for style and colour, so she's absolutely delighted when I remind her about our shopping trip as we break for lunch.

We go into the city centre. As we're wolfing down a bite to eat in a café, Sara pulls her scarf off and holds it up to me, her eyes narrowing.

"Hmmm. I think this is too warm for you," she says.

I'm not exactly sure what she means. It's coral pink, not a colour I'd usually go for. But, truthfully, I don't have a clue. I spend so much of my life in our black-and-white college uniform that I've barely given my wardrobe a thought.

Wrapping the scarf back around her neck, she picks up the menu on our table – a mundane laminated affair – and holds it under my chin.

"Ohhh nice. Okay. Interesting."

"What?"

"Burgundy might be one of yours."

"One of my...?"

"One of your colours. You know, a colour that flatters you. Unlike black. You look like a corpse in that, no offence."

"None taken."

Her eyes scan the room and then our table. She picks up the forest-green napkin beside my plate and opens it out, holding it under my chin.

"Ooh, yes. Forest green. Hmm, I wonder if you're a Summer..."

She could be talking in another language for all I understand.

She narrows her eyes at me. "Still wearing black mascara?"

"Yes."

"You should try navy."

"You really think it'll make a difference?" This isn't the first time she's mentioned it. Make-up shopping hasn't been front of mind lately.

"Yes. We'll get some while we're out. It'll suit you."

The high street is busy, rammed with Christmas shoppers. Sara grabs my arm, and we take shelter in a clothes shop I haven't seen before.

"I think we'll find something in here," she says. "Let's try a few things on."

I love seeing Sara in her zone of genius. She sweeps through the shop, collecting clothes off the rails, and I trail behind her like a little lost child.

She ushers me into a changing room and explains to me her selection. "New coat, three dresses, skirt, two jumpers. I'll figure out shoes and tights once you've tried these on."

"Tights?"

"Yes, Emilie," she says, her voice and posture mimicking a strict schoolmarm. "You don't want to let a perfect outfit down with boring tights."

She certainly seems to have a vision for my look. I go into the cubicle and try on one of the dresses.

"Do you have anything on yet? Come and show me."

I pull back the curtain.

Sara frowns and shakes her head. "That print is too big. Try the lace dress."

As soon as I pull the lace dress over my head, I know I love it. I emerge from the cubicle.

"Yes!" Sara declares, triumphant. "Needs a belt, tights and boots. But that's a winner. What do you think?"

"I love it," I gush.

I end up keeping the cream lace dress, a navy miniskirt in a cute floral print, and one of the jumpers in a delightful forest green. The final thing I try on is a burgundy coat that Sara picked up as soon as we entered the shop. I pull it on and, without looking in the mirror, leave the cubicle.

Sara claps her hands together as though she's praying. "Ohhh yes."

"Is it good?"

"It's fucking fantastic. Look." Sara motions to the huge mirror on the wall beside me. I turn to look at myself.

Ohhhh, okay... I see what she means about burgundy now. After living in black or white for so long, seeing myself in a colour that suits me is like being reanimated. My skin appears smoother; I look healthier. Even my eyes look brighter and more vibrant. And the style is perfect: puff sleeves, pewter buttons down the front, and the shape of the coat means it flatters my natural waist. I look... amazing, frankly.

"Sara, you're a genius."

"I know."

We make our way to the cash register, where Sara hastily adds what she insists are necessary accessories to my pile of clothes: a pretty plaited belt, two pairs of patterned tights and some absolutely gorgeous celestial hairpins. Alongside the rest of the clothes on the counter, I can see they coordinate beautifully.

I shake my head. "Are you sure you don't have some kind of power, some God-given gift you were born with?" I ask, motioning to the pile. Her faux bravado absent for once, she actually blushes. "Seriously, Sara, you should do something with this gift."

"Thank you," she says, giving my arm a squeeze.

We leave the shop, laden with bags, and when Sara suggests taking a look at the market on the high street, I suggest we part ways for a bit.

"I'm just going to grab some underwear," I tell her. "My bras are falling apart. I'll meet you on the high street when I'm done. I won't be long."

Luckily for me, she doesn't argue. I sneak into my favourite lingerie shop, usually reserved for my once-yearly birthday pilgrimage, and scan the racks. I see what I want immediately: a pretty cream lace set. I don't bother trying it on, confident of my size with this brand, and quickly hotfoot it to the high street, where I find Sara standing by the curry stall, eyes half-closed in pleasure as she inhales the scent.

"You can't be hungry – we've just eaten," I tease.

"I'm always hungry for curry," she says, smiling at the cute guy behind the counter.

She glances down at my newly acquired bag and raises an eyebrow but says nothing. I remember her remark about me "taking a lover" and try not to sweat through my T-shirt.

After acquiring a gorgeous pair of lace-up Victorian ankle boots, Sara and I head back to the school via bus. We're both lulled into silence as the coach lumbers along the narrow country lanes, and invariably my mind strays to Tom. Mentally, I review my timetable for the rest of the week and realise we have no lessons together again until the following week. Which means the next time we see each other will be at the train station. My stomach does a backflip.

I turn my face to the window so Sara can't see what I'm thinking. I can't resist mentally revisiting our last encounter in SB.1. But, as I think about that, I'm struck by something I've never considered before: despite the intimate, loving and quite frankly kinky sex we've had, we've never actually properly *kissed*.

Wow.

I sit with this for a moment, allowing it to sink in. We've simply never had the luxury of time or the privacy.

I glance over at Sara and find she's staring at my shopping bags with an odd expression on her face. I feel my stomach lurch.

"You okay?" I ask, breaking her out of her reverie.

"Yup!" she replies, smiling brightly at me. "We did good today, didn't we?"

I smile and nod. "We certainly did."

11

On Saturday morning, I get dressed in my new clothes, and Sara preens as I fuss with my hair in the mirror. I plaited it whilst wet last night and slept in it, so it's now pleasingly wavy. I put most of it up in a tightly braided crown but allow some strands to fall loose.

"Wait, let's try those starry pins you bought," Sara says, and she goes to fetch them. A minute later, and they're in my hair. Small, subtle glints of silver.

"They look great," I say.

She nods, satisfied with her work. "And you're visiting your parents, are you?" she asks.

"Yup," I say, feeling my heart sink. Of course she'd ask that. I look far too dressed up for a visit home. I contemplate lying, fabricating some party I'm going to, but I'm terrified of tying myself in knots I can't keep track of.

"And you're going home for the Christmas break, too?"

"I am."

"Wow, so your family get to see lots of you this month, then," she says, chewing her lip, her eyes not quite meeting mine.

"They do."

I realise now that I should have chosen a different lie. I should have "admitted" to having a boyfriend back home. That would have made this whole ruse a hundred times more believable. Fuck it. Too late now.

I quickly finish packing, wave my roommates goodbye and take my little suitcase to the front of the building, where my taxi is waiting for me.

***

I arrive at the station fifteen minutes early. I study the drivers as cars pass me, but Tom is nowhere to be seen. *He will be here*, I reassure myself. All of this was his idea, after all.

I catch sight of myself in one of the big shiny windows, and my stomach does a funny twist. In my beautiful burgundy coat, my hair dotted with little silver stars, I look so different. I wonder if I've made too much of an effort; if I'm overdressed for the occasion. Urgh.

I glance at my watch, regretting turning up early. All it's done is given me time in which to feel anxious. Just as I'm toying with the idea of sprinting to the bathroom for a final and surely unnecessary nervous wee, I hear footsteps approach.

I turn, and there he is. It's him – undoubtedly – but much like me, he looks completely different in his civvies. He's wearing dark indigo jeans, a smart black wool jacket and a striped scarf in various shades of green.

We stare at each other. There's something going on with his face, something I can't place. I wonder: is it my imagination, or do his eyes look different?

"Hi," I manage.

"Hi," he replies, and finally he smiles at me. "Car's in the short-stay car park."

"Cool."

I'm trying to be cool, but I feel anything but. I'm suddenly shy and awkward in front of him; this all feels so different.

I follow him to the car. He opens the passenger door, and I climb in. Then he places my luggage in the boot, and we're off.

You'd think, having snatched just the tiniest slices of time together this last week, that we'd be talking non-stop for the entire journey. But a strange silence fills the car, and I'm struck dumb. Tom is silent, too, apparently focused on following the satnav, and I just sit there, staring straight ahead.

Eventually I will myself to talk, and I ask the question that's been swirling around my head since we set off.

"What did you think when you saw me today?" I ask, butterflies fluttering in my stomach.

His face softens into a smile. "How beautiful you look," he replies softly, and my heart all but floats out of my chest. The free-floating anxiety that's been tormenting me since this morning is immediately quelled by his words.

We fall silent yet again. I think about the fact that we haven't actually *kissed* yet. I expect Tom to say something, because surely he can hear my thoughts, but he doesn't, and I don't have the courage to ask out loud. We pass the big blue "Welcome to Scotland" sign.

Soon, the landscape changes, and we're treated to verdant hills and big blue-grey stretches of water as the coastline comes into view. My excitement builds. Aside from the luxury of having time with Tom, I'm genuinely thrilled to be in Scotland, exploring this new land.

The next thought that pops into my head is an unwelcome one and, given Tom's telepathy, not one I want to entertain within "earshot" of him. But I can't help myself, and I wonder: has he done all of this with someone else?

"I haven't, Emilie, no," he says gently, and he reaches over and gives my hand a little squeeze.

"Sorry."

"Don't apologise. It's only natural to be curious."

"Have you... had many girlfriends?"

"I was in a long-term relationship at university, but it didn't work out. It was fun, but I think we both knew it wouldn't last."

I nod. "Were you in love?"

"I thought I was. Looking back now, I don't think so. But we cared about one another." He removes his hand from mine in order to change gear.

"Did she know about the telepathy?"

"No."

"Oh!" I'm surprised by this. "Who does know?"

"Just you and my parents. And my sister. Growing up, I thought everyone could hear everyone else's thoughts. With the help of my parents, it dawned on me that they couldn't."

I try and fail to imagine how wild that must have been for Tom's family. "How do you think the rumour about you started at school?"

"I have no idea. I can only assume it was a lucky guess. Perhaps another telepath, as unlikely as that would be. But I'd have heard their thoughts about me if that were the case."

"Is it hereditary, the telepathy?"

"Possibly. Mum and Dad don't have it, but it was rumoured that one of my great uncles was a telepath. So perhaps it does run in the family."

Something occurs to me – something I've been meaning to ask. "How close do you need to be to someone to hear their thoughts?"

"Depends. Some thoughts are louder than others. But usually a metre or two. And most of the time it's like overhearing a telephone conversation, just snippets of inner monologue. But dreams and daydreams tend to be more visual, as you know..."

I detect the smile in his words.

Tom exits the A1. I don't think anything of this until I glance at the satnav, which says that we've got another 30 minutes of driving to do before we reach our destination.

"Are we here?" I ask, confused, as we pull into a little car park.

"Not yet. We can't check in until this afternoon. Figured we'd take a little detour."

"Is this the part where you murder me and bury my body in the middle of nowhere?"

Tom laughs. "It would be remiss not to make the most of the opportunity."

We climb out of the car, and it's only as I stand that I see the view in front of us.

Holy shit.

A vast beach stretches out before us, a wide crescent of rich golden sand bordered by long green grass. As we make our way onto the beach, I see that the tide is out, and the remaining water creates a huge mirror, reflecting the nearly cloudless sky.

I'm dumbfounded. The beaches I grew up near were small, touristy and heaving with lobster-red bodies in the summer. They were nothing like this – incomparable in sheer size and raw, devastating beauty. Better still, there's literally no one here.

Loose strands of hair whip my face. I'm gawping. I even forget, just for a moment, that Tom's here with me, holding my hand and leading me towards the water. I take it all in: the hills on the horizon, the seemingly infinite ocean, the taste of salt on my lips.

"Wow," I breathe, and I finally turn to look at him. He's wearing the broadest smile I've ever seen, his dark chocolate eyes creased at the corners.

"This is" – I gesture with my free hand – "breathtaking," I manage eventually.

"As are you," he says, taking both of my hands now, and suddenly my attention is fully on him. His affection for me shines out of his face, almost blinding me. My stomach completes a full triple backflip.

"Emilie, I love you. I wanted to wait until the right moment to tell you. I wanted it to be special."

He pulls me closer, but I remain speechless, even though I want to reply because I know exactly what to say. He places my hands on his waist, cups my face and then, after a second's pause, he kisses me.

I'm aware of everything: his soft lips, the lightness of his touch, his warm hands on my cold face. This kiss, it's unhurried, careful, infused with so much feeling. This, I realise, *this* is what it's like to be loved. I feel it, in him, in the way he kisses me and in my own heart, which now feels far too big for my ribcage.

A dog barks in the distance, and we pull apart, no longer alone.

He doesn't say anything, and neither do I; we just beam inanely at each other in that positively vomit-inducing way new lovers do. To any passing observer, we're just a random loved-up couple kissing on a beach.

He strokes my wayward hair off my face, cups the nape of my neck with his warm fingers. "We've got an hour before we check in. Do you want to explore the town?"

I beam. "Yes, I do."

12

It's only as we head towards the nearest town that I realise I'm starving. I haven't eaten since this morning, and it's well past midday. Tom seems to know exactly where to go, though. He takes my hand and tells me he found a great place we can eat. I've never been with someone so thoughtful and organised before and, honestly, I bloody love it.

The architecture is different here: rectangular buildings with grey slate roofs and ornate sandstone walls. It's cold but sunny. Given it's a Saturday in December, the town isn't too busy. We walk past a gift shop and, without meaning to, I stop dead outside it, bowled over by what I see. In the window is a beautiful cream Aran jumper, the criss-cross of a Celtic knot down the front, with an unusual boat neck that indicates it was made for a woman. It's delicate, pretty, not your usual fisherman's jumper. It would look great with the floral miniskirt I bought with Sara on Wednesday.

I suddenly remember where I am.

"Sorry," I say to Tom, who was holding my hand and therefore had to stop, too. I glimpse at the price tag before I will myself into motion again. It's beautiful, but it's well out of my price range, and I feel slightly embarrassed knowing that Tom might have heard all that contemplation over a jumper, of all things.

"Okay?" he asks.

I smile and nod. He doesn't mention anything about the jumper – perhaps he didn't hear those thoughts – and we continue walking until we reach the café.

It's both gorgeous and unusual, tucked up in the loft of a big stone building with terracotta tiles on the roof. Tom, still holding my hand, leads me up a stone staircase and into the café, where we're presented with the most delightful array of cakes and bakes.

Ten minutes later, I'm tucking into a huge butternut squash salad. I'm alone, just for a moment; Tom has gone to wash his hands, and I take the opportunity to wolf down my food, starving as I am, with the intention of being far more elegant (and less like the Cookie Monster) when Tom returns.

I admire the café as I eat, with its lovely mismatched oak furniture, teal walls and beautiful local paintings. On the wall furthest from me hangs a giant silver fork and spoon. The winter sun is shining through the skylights, the food is delicious and it occurs to me that I'm just so happy right now. This was a perfect choice for lunch, and I can't wait to see our accommodation. The man clearly has great taste.

Tom takes longer than I was expecting in the loo, I hope he's okay. When he returns, he looks a little flushed.

"Sorry, I got accosted by a very friendly Scottish woman wanting a chat," he says as he sits down. "I didn't want to be rude."

"Well, that's adorable," I say. "You couldn't disappoint her, could you?"

"No, quite." Tom looks at my plate and smiles. "Hungry?"

"Starving, as you well know," I tease. "This place was an excellent choice for lunch, by the way."

"Glad you think so," he says, and I'm treated to one of his enormous smiles.

After lunch, we spend a couple of hours exploring the town and the surrounding area. We walk along the River Tyne, holding hands, and I can't resist pointing out all the cute dogs I see. It's such a reflex action of mine, so it's only after the fifth dog that I wonder if this is actually a really irritating habit for others to endure. Tom laughs at this and assures me it's not.

There's a notable drop in temperature as we approach late afternoon, and I'm grateful when Tom suggests we head to our accommodation. He hasn't said anything about where he's booked, and I'm impatient to see it.

We drive up a hill, up a little private road, and I'm so distracted by the stunning views of the sea in the wing mirror that I nearly don't notice the cottage right in front of us. We park out front, and I immediately understand why Tom booked it; the little white house with its slate roof is pretty typical for the area, but the front of the building is largely glass, making the most of the glorious vista. It's perfect.

"Oh wow," I sigh as Tom parks the car.

He turns to look at me, a smile on his face. "Why don't you take a look?" he says, handing me some keys. "I'll bring the cases in."

Like a child, I unlock the door and rush inside.

13

Oh my God.

It's the very essence of tasteful: a neutral colour scheme with wooden floors and pale oak furniture. In the corner, a tall branch is wrapped in fairy lights, and flokati rugs are artfully arranged near soft grey armchairs. I greedily take in the small but perfectly formed kitchen and dining area before hastily kicking off my boots and hotfooting it up the stairs.

I'm not at all prepared for what I see.

The big puffy bed catches my eye first, a veritable cloud in the centre of the room, but as I reach the top of the stairs, I quite literally gasp as I see the colours of the twilight through the vast glass pane in the roof. A silver sliver of moon is high in the pinky-purple sky, the horizon a soft, glowing orange.

I hear Tom climb the stairs and I turn to face him. The light of the golden hour catches his features. My eyes are wide like saucers.

"What do you think?" he asks, carefully placing our cases down.

Winded by the view, I can barely draw a breath to reply.

"It's so beautiful. So, so beautiful. Oh my God. Thank you."

He takes a few steps towards me and wraps me in a bear hug, pulling me tightly against him. I wrap myself around him, tighter still, and inhale his scent; lime, pine, sandalwood. There's every risk I may die of happiness.

"I'm so glad you like it," he says softly into my hair. "I wanted it to be perfect for you."

I pull away slightly so I can look him in the eye. "It's amazing. I'm not sure what my expectations were, but you've exceeded them in every single way," I say earnestly.

"I have a little something for you."

My eyebrows hit my hairline. "Really? As if all of this isn't enough?"

He looks a little sheepish as he walks over to our cases and retrieves a large, fancy-looking gift bag, which I accept from him, stunned. Perched on the edge of the bed, I rustle through the pale blue tissue paper to find the stunning cream jumper I'd been admiring only hours ago. Sweet Jesus. There's a very real risk I might implode.

I flop back onto the whisper-soft duvet, hugging the beautiful jumper to my chest. "Tom, this is too much."

"Emilie, please let me. I wanted you to have a souvenir from our trip. I was planning on getting you a little something anyway."

"Thank you. I really wanted it," I say, his thoughtfulness making my eyes prickle.

"I know you did."

"When on earth did you— Oh. There was no chatty old lady, was there?"

"No," he says, and he actually giggles, which is adorable.

I let out a long sigh as I sink back into the bed, staring up at the sky. Perhaps it's just that I'm not used to this kind of treatment. Never have I been with someone so painstakingly thoughtful.

"Try it on," he urges, giving me a gentle nudge.

I stand and pull it on over the dress I'm wearing, then walk over to the full-length mirror beside the bed. The jumper fits perfectly. Wow. It's a solid eleven out of ten and goes perfectly with the cream lace dress I'm wearing. Sara is going to be *so* happy for me.

I run my hand over the intricate cables, admiring all the work that's gone into it. It's handmade, for sure. Tom flicks on the bedside light and then comes and stands behind me, his cheek resting against my hair.

"It looks so good on you," he says, meeting my gaze in the mirror.

"It's perfect," I say. "I don't think I'll ever take it off."

The corners of his mouth curl into a grin, and our eyes meet. Tenderness is etched all over his features, and his expression hits me right in the heart.

His black-brown eyes are studying my face in the mirror. I watch him smile again, then he breathes a contented sigh and turns to kiss my neck. I notice he doesn't close his eyes, that he continues to watch me in the mirror as I respond to him, his pupils big and dark. Then he turns and buries his face in my hair, kissing my ear, moving his fingers up to massage my scalp.

I close my eyes, lost in sensation, marvelling at the way he knows exactly what I like. We've been so time-poor that this kind of slow, indulgent touching has been off limits until now. I wonder if, even without the telepathy, he would know just what I want.

And then it hits me: we're here, alone, just the two of us, this entire cottage to ourselves. Cosy, private, delightfully warm.

"I want you to know there's no expectation, Emilie," he says, his face still in my hair. "Just because we're here, it doesn't mean..."

God. Those words. I'm speechless. Whilst I have every intention of making the absolute most of our time together in whatever way Tom will allow, it's shockingly sexy to know that nothing's expected.

"There is one thing, though," he says, turning to look at my reflection again.

The mirror informs me that I've failed to hide my surprise. "What's that?"

"I'd love to see you with your hair down," he says. "I don't think I ever have."

I smile. What a sweet request.

"Of course."

I hastily pull the pins from my hair, placing them on the bedside table, then wrestle my mane out of its plaited crown. It tumbles down, extra wavy now from being bound up so tight.

He sighs again, a smile dancing on his lips. "You're so beautiful."

I shake my head, my gaze immediately dropping to the floor. It isn't that I think I'm some hideous wildebeest, simply that taking a compliment has never been my forte.

He starts to play with my hair, his knuckles brushing against my back as he does so. Then his fingers are on my neck as he makes a loose ponytail, gently pulling it tight, and my entire body relaxes as I fall into a trance. I can't remember the last time someone touched my hair like this. I close my eyes, feeling the most pleasurable tingling sensation run up my spine and spread across the back of my skull.

"Do you want to lie down?" he asks.

I nod, opening my eyes and meeting my gaze in the mirror. It's not that I'm sleepy; it's that he's somehow hypnotised me, and my muscles have turned to jelly. The cloud-bed looks more inviting than ever.

"Can I undress you first?" he asks my reflection.

I nod again, dumbfounded, and turn to face him. But, to my surprise, he turns me back to face the mirror. "Let me show you how beautiful you are."

My face heats at his words. He removes my jumper first, and I feel a little sheepish, childlike even, as he pulls it over my head. We both laugh as it gets stuck, and I have to wiggle myself free.

I reach down to pull off my tights, feeling self-conscious about them and wondering whether I should have worn something sexier, when Tom catches my wrist and stops me.

"There's no rush, Emilie," he says softly. "And trust me, you have absolutely *nothing* to worry about."

His hands move under my skirt, coming to rest on my hips before he reaches up and slowly, so slowly, eases my tights down. I step out of them as gracefully as I can.

His attention returns to me. He unzips the back of my dress and slips a hand inside to stroke my back. His unhurried focus, the way he's so obviously savouring this, turns me on so much.

"Look," he says.

I'd forgotten about the mirror. I glance at myself, noticing the subtle way my face has softened, how my eyes are black and my cheeks are pink.

He gently moves the hair from my shoulder and plants a light kiss there, and then another, and another, working his way up my neck. I lean into him, arching my back, wanting more. But instead he pulls away, his hands sliding under the dress and up to my shoulders. With one quick move, it falls to the floor.

"Oh my God, Emilie," he says, bowing his head as if in prayer. Then, for several moments, he just looks at me as though I'm Venus emerging from her giant seashell.

His lips return to my shoulder to kiss it, but his eyes meet mine in the mirror, his expression tormented. His hand is still on my back, and he trails his fingertips up my spine, making me shiver with pleasure.

The light in the room is beautiful; the soft glow of the bedside lamp and the setting sun. I'm deeply relaxed, my body soft. And so incredibly turned on by how gentle he is with me.

"What do you want, Emilie?" he asks softly, his lips against my hair as he gazes at my reflection.

I want more of this. I want him to stroke me, to tease me. I want him to make me beg.

"I want your hands on me," I say.

His little grunt-sigh lets me know he got all of that, loud and clear. He wraps his arms around me at first, pulling me back towards him. His erection, hard and urgent, pushes against my lower back, and his hands sweep over my abdomen before moving up to cup my breasts. As he pinches my nipples through the fine material of my bra, I lean back, pressing into him.

He lets out a heavy sigh. Despite his insistence that there's no need to rush, I can tell he's struggling. In a second, he's unhooked my bra and it's on the floor. With one hand caressing my naked breast, he slides the other into the back of my knickers, cupping my buttock.

"Oh God," he huffs, sounding pained.

I reach behind me, finding his rock-hard cock, and stroke it through his trousers. He responds with a moan, and I study his face in the mirror, his pleasure clearly evident.

I turn towards him and begin to unzip his trousers. He lets me, and I wrestle with his clothes until both his trousers and boxers are on the floor. He kicks off his socks, whips off his shirt and motions for me to lie on the bed.

I do, and when he lies on top of me, I'm torn. I want this so badly, the weight of him on me, the feeling of him inside me, but I also want to study and admire his naked body. He smiles and turns his head towards the mirror. I look and see our reflection in it. At some point, unbeknown to me, he must have angled the mirror towards the bed.

Christ. Seeing our bodies entwined like this, his naked bottom, the way he's lying on top of me, his arms either side of my head... I wiggle out of his grasp and reach down to yank off my knickers, all pretence of patience gone.

"Please," I pant, parting my legs.

I've never seen a man put on a condom so quickly.

He slides inside me and begins to thrust. I cry out, so close already, and look at the mirror again, admiring the way he's buried inside me, our hips glued together, his muscles straining.

I turn again so I can study his beautiful face. He's flushed, his breathing hard and fast. He kisses me, sliding his tongue gently into my mouth, mirroring what's going on between my legs.

When we need to break for air, I plead with him. "More. Please."

"Uhh, Emilie," he pants, pushing himself all the way into me.

I writhe in pleasure, twisting my hips from side to side, feeling the way he fills me. More. I want more. And I want him to come; I want to see him fall apart.

He's setting the pace. Urgent, deep, firm but not rough. It's precisely the speed and pressure I need. We come together, and as we do, he cries out my name. It's everything I've ever wanted.

Afterwards, as we lie together, his hand lazily stroking my back, I finally tell him that I love him.

He turns to me and smiles, happiness radiating from him in big, luxurious waves.

"I know, Emilie," he says simply. "I know."

14

I WAKE FAR TOO early.

The dark of the night is just starting to lift, the sky a pale, electric blue. In the shadows, I can make out Tom's face; the faint beginnings of a beard, mussed-up hair, long dark eyelashes. He's so quiet that, for a second, I wonder if he's even breathing.

But he is. And, as if sensing my laser-like stare, his eyes flutter open. Immediately, he grins.

"Morning." His voice is thick with sleep.

"Morning," I reply. I start to wiggle towards him from beneath the cloud-duvet, and he opens his arms. I slide into them, my skin coming into contact with his as our naked bodies collide, and feel a literal hit of oxytocin flood my brain.

"Guhh," I moan, imitating an affection-starved zombie.

Tom squeezes me even tighter, burying his face into my neck and making appreciative noises of his own. "Mmmm, Emilie."

I'll never tire of hearing him say my name.

We lie there, still, sleep-warmed bodies pressed tightly together. I think in clichés: about how I never want this to end, how if I died right now I'd be happy.

I trail my fingertips down Tom's spine, my hand coming to rest on his perfectly round buttock, and immediately flash back to last night. His hands cradling my hips, the weight of him as he slid between my legs. The striking image of us both writhing against each other in the mirror.

I feel something stir against my hip; hear Tom's quiet but unmistakable sigh.

"Are you reading my thoughts again?"

A short laugh. "Yes. Sorry. Tired."

I grin. "Bad man."

"I am."

My hand snakes round to the front of his thigh. I play with the light smattering of hair I find there.

"I have a suitable punishment." My fingers creep towards his burgeoning erection.

His breathing changes. "What's that?"

I take hold of his cock. "Tell me again about that time my lascivious thoughts nearly derailed your lesson..."

An hour later, when I emerge from the bathroom, Tom's nowhere to be seen. I venture downstairs to find him in the kitchen.

"Hot chocolate? Coffee? Mocha?" he offers, looking up as I approach. I spot the brown paper bags on the counter. My stomach rumbles.

"Ooh. Mocha, please."

I start to approach, but he ushers me away.

"Take a seat. I'll bring it over."

I sit on a wooden bench covered in soft grey cushions. The view is out of this world: an expanse of hammered steel-grey water surrounded by mountains that are soft purple in the early morning light. There's only a smattering of clouds above the horizon, and they're far off in the distance, tucked neatly behind the mountains.

Tom appears beside me, drink in hand, and places the most decadent, flaky croissant I've ever seen in front of me.

I look at him with unbridled adoration. "Have I told you how much I love you?" I simper.

He laughs. "You have. This morning, in fact. Several times, if I remember correctly."

Ah yes. My cheeks colour despite myself.

We fall into a reverential silence as we eat and take in the view. I'm aware that I'm soaking up every last detail of this trip for later. I'll need them all to sustain me.

"When do we have to leave?"

"In about an hour."

My heart sinks. "What's next?"

"Lunch? A walk?"

"No, I mean..."

He smiles. "I knew what you meant." He looks thoughtful. "We should arrange when and where to meet."

"Should we... swap numbers?" It seems like an almost absurd thing to suggest given our relationship status.

He shakes his head. "Our phones will be the first thing the police seize if we ever get caught. Even having your number on me is a risk. Let's not take that chance."

He's right, of course. "Okay."

We discuss locations, agree that meeting up immediately after term ends and before he's officially started at his new school is risky. So we pick a date in January; the first weekend after the spring term starts.

"Christ. That's weeks away," I whine.

"I know." He pulls me into his arms. "But let's not think about that now. Let's make the most of the time we have left."

I climb onto his lap, nuzzling into him, and he starts to stroke my hair.

"God, I love you so much, Emilie." His voice cracks.

His words have the power to recharge me, to erase all anxiety I have about the future.

"I love you, too."

15

We return Sunday night after dark, arriving at the campus separately so as not to arouse suspicion. I can sense, as the taxi approaches, that the college feels different. *I* feel different. I'm not the same person who left here yesterday morning. I'm bolstered, renewed, restored by our trip away. This morning already feels like a lifetime ago.

Sara is white-faced as she meets me at the door, and immediately I know something's wrong. She looks around as if to check no one can hear us before she speaks.

"They know, Emilie."

"Know what?"

She takes me by the arm and steers me into the games room, which is, thankfully, empty.

"About you. And Mr Wakefield."

Fuck.

Fuck, fuck, fuck.

I pause for a moment too long. "What are you on about? There is no me and Mr Wakefield. In my dreams, sure. But that's it."

Sara rolls her eyes. "You must think I'm stupid."

"I have a boyfriend at home," I blurt out, remembering the excuse I should have used before I left. "That's why I wanted to go shopping. That's why I got dressed up to go home."

"If you had a boyfriend at home, I'd know about it. There's no way you'd have kept that from me."

She's right, of course.

"There's no me and Mr Wakefield," I repeat. I know I'm gaslighting her, but I have no choice. The stakes are simply too high.

She crosses her arms, clearly angry. "I know you're bullshitting me, but I'm going to overlook that for now. The point is the rumour mill has been rabid since you left. I don't know who started it, but I want you to know it wasn't me."

I'm stunned into silence. Not only does Sara know, but so does the entire fucking school apparently. Shit. How on earth did this happen? Did someone see us?

"How? Who? What evidence do they think they have? This has to have come from somewhere."

"No idea where it's come from. But literally everyone's talking about it. Ms Kirby has been issuing detentions over it."

"Fuck." I'm shaking. "He could lose his job if people believe that shit."

Sara's expression is grim. "I know."

I don't go and hang out in the common room with the others. Instead, I go straight to my room to unpack and digest this fucking disaster. Sara doesn't join me. She's pissed that I won't admit to her what's going on, and I feel terrible, but I have bigger fish to fry.

I don't know what to do, and I don't sleep that night, although I pretend to doze off early to avoid questions from my roommates. All I can think about, as I lie in bed while everyone else is sleeping, is how close to freedom we were.

16

On Monday, I'm subject to odd looks and hushed voices as I navigate my way around college. Sara is still angry with me, and I don't know what to do about that. I'm exhausted and pale; I struggle to eat. I trowel on make-up, trying to look more alive and less guilty, and I wonder how I'd behave if the rumour wasn't true. Would I have been able to laugh it off? Would I behave differently? Can those around me smell my guilt?

I wonder if Tom is privy to this gossip. If he hasn't overheard it, then surely a teacher – Ms Kirby perhaps – would have told him. I wonder how he's feeling, how he's coping.

Having avoided it all morning, I eventually brave the common room and regret it immediately. Sara wasn't exaggerating. When I enter, the room becomes noticeably quieter. Fuck.

I sidle up to Sara, dragging a chair next to hers when I see there isn't one available. She gives me one of her looks.

"Tea?" I offer.

She shakes her head, sullen.

"Digestive?"

She ignores me.

"Chocolate digestive?"

She sighs, holding out her hand. "Go on then."

I lay the biscuit on her hand as though I'm crossing a fortune teller's palm with silver.

"Did you hear about Becky's latest incident?" I try, offering up this little nugget of gossip as an olive branch.

This gets her attention. She narrows her eyes. "No..."

"She tried to use magic to do lip fillers. On her own face."

Sara's eyebrows shoot up to meet her hairline. "Are you serious?"

"Deadly serious. She was mysteriously absent for a few days. Apparently she looked like she'd been stung by a swarm of bees. The nurse was furious."

I have Sara's attention now. Her eyes are sparkling. "Holy shit. That's absolutely amazing."

I feel a tiny bit bad. As a rule, I don't like to gossip about anyone, but surely the current circumstances could be considered exceptional.

Sara's halfway through her third biscuit and I'm just returning from the water cooler when I overhear a conversation that makes my heart stop.

"Did you hear about the ex-teacher that was jailed for three years after having a relationship with a pupil?"

"Oh my God. Did he work here?"

"Yeah. Years ago."

I have no doubt this conversation is being had well within my earshot for my benefit. But still, it sends my stomach plummeting.

"He got put on the Sex Offenders Register for the rest of his life."

"Wow, didn't know that. Was she underage, then?"

"No, she was over the age of consent. But it's still considered abuse if it's a relationship between a pupil and a teacher."

I don't turn around. I refuse to acknowledge this. But I need to return to my seat because I'm worried I might actually faint.

I slump into my chair, legs trembling. In my periphery, I'm aware that Sara is staring at me.

Fuck.

PRISON?

Why has this not occurred to me before now?

WHY HAS THIS NOT OCCURRED TO ME BEFORE NOW?

Fucking hell.

Fucking. HELL.

I think I might throw up.

On our way to our next lesson, Sara forcefully shoves me into the toilet, and I nearly collide with a girl who's on her way out. She shoots me a filthy look as we pass.

"You look unhinged," Sara says when she's sure there's no one else in here.

"Fuck."

"It's not just a rumour, is it?"

I cling to the white porcelain sink, sure I'm going to be sick.

"No," I manage, my whole body trembling.

"I fucking knew it."

"I'm sorry."

She sighs. "I don't blame you for lying. I'm just insulted you didn't think I'd cotton on."

"Was it that obvious?"

"Only to me. I knew you lied about your period. And I knew the fancy underwear wasn't for visiting your parents. And… I couldn't shake the feeling that *something* was going on."

"I guess you weren't the only one," I say. I'm shaking so violently. God only knows what someone would think if they walked in on us right now.

Sara rests a hand on my arm. "I'm sorry it got out. I have no idea how. I suppose someone else must have twigged. You didn't do anything silly on campus, did you?"

I close my eyes. It's all the answer she needs.

"Wow, Emilie. That was risky."

"It was stupid. We both were."

"Where?"

I open my eyes. "You really want all the details? Now?"

"Sorry," she says, looking sheepish. "Inappropriate."

I can't help but smile despite myself. "Fuck it," I whisper. "It looks like we're going down anyway so… We had sex, here, at the college. After class. And it was fucking amazing. You can't tell a soul."

Sara's hands fly to her mouth. "Emilie!" I can tell she's grinning behind her hands. "Oh my God. It was amazing?"

"Life-affirming, life-changing, all that stuff. Undoubtedly the best sex I'll ever have. Even better than my fantasies."

"Bloody hell..." She's awestruck. But then her expression suddenly changes to something more serious. "Could you have been seen?"

"If we were, I had no idea." I glance at myself in the mirror, hair wild, mascara smudged. Sara wasn't kidding when she said I looked unhinged.

"I'm so scared, Sar. I'm terrified he'll go to prison and get put on the Sex Offenders Register."

I'm desperate for her to tell me I'm being ridiculous, that I'm catastrophising, as she so often does. Not this time.

"God, you look terrible," she says instead.

"Sorry," I mutter, sprinting into a cubicle. "Gonna be sick."

17

The following afternoon I'm due to have a lesson with Tom. It's Tuesday, we haven't seen each other since the weekend and we've had precisely zero opportunity to talk. I desperately try and gauge his mood as I walk into the room, but his perfect poker face gives nothing away. It's a shame I'm not telepathic.

I try to act normal. I try to keep my shit together. I try not to think about the conversation I overheard in the common room yesterday. I sit at the front, next to Sara, and halfway through the lesson, shit gets real weird.

First, Ms Kirby stops by, casually leaning against the door frame. I hazard a guess at her age. She must be at least a decade older than Tom.

"Your final week then, Mr Wakefield?" she trills. She's wearing a red top, loud floral skirt and a blue beaded necklace that looks as though it might have come from a child's dressing-up box.

"Yes, Ms Kirby," he replies, giving her a smile.

I recognise the tension behind it. He just wants to be done with this small talk. Although we've never discussed it, it's clear to me he doesn't like this woman, and I'm suddenly desperate to know why.

"Will you be celebrating after work on Friday?"

Tom seems uncharacteristically uncomfortable with this line of questioning. I notice he's fiddling with his shirt cuffs.

"Not sure yet."

Ms Kirby looks surprised. "Well, if you do, let me know. I'd love to join you."

With a tight smile, Tom does this weird half-nod that isn't actually a nod at all. Thankfully, Ms Kirby seems to get the hint.

"Good luck in your new job, Tom."

"Thanks."

She leaves. All at once, everyone starts to talk, and Tom has to quieten the class.

"Don't make me give you a detention in the last week of term," he threatens.

Although we all know he wouldn't, the threat seems to work. There's some whispering and curious glances, but the class does settle down. What was that? Was she asking Tom out for a drink? Although the conversation seemed professional, I can't shake the feeling there was another unspoken exchange going on there. Has she asked him out before? Is there history between them? What could I have missed?

Then, as if the lesson couldn't get any weirder, my fellow classmate – Becky, of course – gets to her feet.

"Mr Wakefield, will you go out with me?"

What.

The.

Fuck.

Has she been drinking? Actually, judging by her ruddy complexion, shiny eyes and ridiculous grin, that's well within the realms of possibility.

Tom looks as though he's really fucking had enough of today. What with the rumour circulating about us, Ms Kirby being weird and now this. Jesus H Christ will someone give this man a break.

"Rebecca," he says, to make a point, "whilst I'm flattered, you and I both know that it would be entirely inappropriate and unethical. I don't date my students."

"But what about Emilie?"

The entire class goes silent; everyone's holding their breath. I'm certain I'm going to be sick again. The effort required not to vomit from sheer terror is unlike anything I've ever experienced. My eyes start to water.

Tom, cool as a cucumber, rolls his eyes, casual as you like. "That's pure fiction. Honestly, I don't know what's got into everyone lately. I announce I'm leaving, and the gossip mill starts. I don't know who started the rumour, but I will find out."

I'm completely in awe of his acting skills. Seriously, give this man an Oscar.

"Becky, Emilie, stay behind after class."

Oh.

Becky and I remain as the class files from the room. Tom has us move to the front so he can address us properly.

"Rumours about me dating a pupil could ruin my career. I hope for your sake, Becky, that you haven't been responsible for spreading them."

She remains silent, her gaze firmly on the dusty parquet flooring.

"Firstly, I think you should apologise to Emilie."

Her nostrils flare. "Sorry."

She certainly doesn't sound it.

Tom continues. "Secondly: your proposition to me was entirely inappropriate. Do you understand?"

She nods, sullen, her jaw set. I notice her neck is starting to turn red.

"You can leave."

Ouch. I almost feel sorry for her.

Becky stands up, chair scraping on the floor as she does so, and storms out of the room.

I'm silent, stony. I don't dare look at him. Already he'll know something's up because now, with Becky gone, I'm still refusing to look at him.

"Emilie?" Tom says, very quietly. I can hear the worry in his voice. And I think about how risky it would be for us to have an actual conversation right now. The door is open – he can't be seen to even close it.

You could be jailed for this, I think as clearly as I can so that he can hear me. *We can't afford to be seen together.*

He says nothing, but my skin prickles as I sense him edge towards me. He might be the telepath, but I know exactly what he's thinking.

You could end up on the Sex Offenders Register for the rest of your life. You'd never teach again. Do you understand?

I stand up. I have to go. We can't be seen together like this.

My gaze remains firmly on the battered wooden desk as I fumble with my things. Tom is completely silent, unnervingly so. I'm clumsy as I collect my bag, fighting with the strap as I put it on my shoulder. My eyes flick to him for a split second. He looks pale, jaw set, eyes shinier than usual, and my heart aches for him. Why does this have to be so hard? So complicated?

I force my face into a more neutral expression and turn away from him. Head down, heart breaking, I march out of the room.

18

I don't sleep that night. The following morning, Sara hovers round me like an anxious mother. At breakfast, in the canteen, she hands me a banana as she loiters beside me.

"You have to eat something," she insists.

I feel sick at the thought. "I'm trying," I mutter.

She wanders off again and returns moments later with a croissant before settling herself opposite me. I manage a few mouthfuls of flaky pastry between sips of weak tea.

"Three more days left of term," Sara says in a hushed voice, doing her best to reassure me. "Just three more days. That's all."

I nod, forcing another mouthful of banana down me. I'm so focused on not throwing up that I don't notice a teacher approach me.

"Emilie?"

I leap out of my skin. Jesus. Could I look any guiltier?

It's Ms Kirby. "The head wants to see you in his office," she says.

"Okay," I reply, trying to keep my voice light. I glance up at her as she walks away. I can't read her expression; it's carefully neutral.

I put my half-eaten banana down on my tray, hands shaking. I don't need to say anything.

"I'll walk with you," Sara says.

En route we make a quick pit stop. I'm grateful the toilets are empty. I stare at myself in the mirror; I barely recognise the woman staring back at me.

Sara rummages in her bag. "Try this." She hands me a lipstick. "It'll make your lips look less pale."

I apply it. It helps, I think.

She hands me another item from her bag. "These will help with your red eyes."

I use the eye drops and reassess myself. She's right – they seem to work. I rake my brush through my hair and study myself. I look marginally more human and a tad less unstable.

"What are you going to say?" Sara asks. She doesn't ask me what it is I think I'm being called in for. We both know. It couldn't possibly be anything else.

"I have no idea, Sar," I say. "I haven't had a chance to think about it." Will they call Tom in too? Should we have pre-empted this and got our stories straight? Too late now.

"You can't tell them, surely..." she says. She looks worried, which does nothing for my nervous stomach. It's rare to see her concerned about anything.

"No, you're right. I can't. If Tom admits to it and I lie, I get into trouble for lying. Big deal. But if I admit it and Tom doesn't, his career is over." I feel myself start to crumple. "Fuck. Fuck, fuck, fuck."

She grabs me by the shoulders. "Stay focused. Come on. You can do this. You have to."

"I know," I say, trying to swallow back tears. "I know."

When I arrive at the head's office, Tom is outside wearing the same expression I saw yesterday – jaw tense, eyes shiny. Pale. He doesn't even look at me.

The door opens. "Good. You're here. Come in."

I follow Tom into the dark-panelled room. Bookshelves line the walls. We lower ourselves into chairs placed in front of an imposing walnut desk.

The head – Mr Montgomery – leans forward in his black leather chair.

"I suspect you both know why I've had to call you in today. As I'm sure you're aware, there's a rumour circulating about a relationship between the two of you."

I swallow, too terrified to speak. Tom remains silent, too. I stare at the beautiful amethyst crystal floating in a glass jar on a shelf behind Mr Montgomery's head.

"Should I be concerned?" he prompts.

"Absolutely not," Tom says, at the same time I say, "No!"

Tom continues. "I've no idea where this unfounded rumour has come from, and I'm concerned it could jeopardise my new job."

"Can you think why anyone would want to start such a rumour?"

"I wish I knew," Tom says. "The timing's terrible."

Mr Montgomery slowly nods, impassive. "I hope you'll understand that I need to investigate this allegation. Particularly given... past events. I can't be seen to ignore this."

Tom swallows. "I understand."

Fuck.

"The process is already in motion," Mr Montgomery continues. "Given the timing, I had no choice. But I want a prompt resolution, given how close we are to the end of term. I'll speak to you again on Friday afternoon. If no one's come forward with any proof, then we can chalk this up as malicious tittle-tattle, and no one needs to hear any more about it."

We both nod, expressions grim.

"Emilie, you've been very quiet. Do you have anything to say on the matter?" Mr Montgomery prompts.

I shake my head. "What is there to say? Someone's spreading rumours about us."

"Any classmates with a grudge? Anyone who would be motivated to start this?"

"None that I can think of."

"Okay." He leans back in his chair, seeming satisfied. "We'll talk again at the end of the week."

19

IF ONLY WE'D WAITED. If only we'd been more careful. It's impossible to know whether we were seen or whether someone is making this up. Perhaps the rumour would have started even if we hadn't been seeing each other. I think about our first romantic encounter in the observatory. If only we'd agreed then to wait. If only we'd had some semblance of self-control. If only Tom hadn't dropped to his knees and made me see the sun and the moon and the stars even though, in that moment, it's what I so desperately wanted.

Would it have made a difference had we waited? Technically, yes. And perhaps the rumour mill wouldn't have started; perhaps we could have safely dated in the New Year with a clean slate and clear consciences. Tom, no longer a teacher at my college, no longer in a position of power with me as his student. Surely that would have been okay? Perhaps, had we just held our nerve, we could have survived.

I think about how risky it would be to see him even after term ends. What if someone from the school sees us? Could he be jailed still? Retrospectively? What if someone from my college goes to the same university and sees us together? Puts two and two together? Figures out the rumours were true? And why didn't I think about all this before now? My impatience, my overwhelming desire for him, has got me into this mess. Had we just waited...

It's Thursday, the penultimate day of term. Today, we await our fate. Tomorrow, we find out whether our lives are ruined forever. I'm sick as a pig, riddled with anxiety.

As the day draws to a close, I retch bile in the empty toilet block and cry silently in what little privacy I can find. I miss my last lesson, desperately trying to collect myself.

As I emerge from the toilets into the empty corridor, I'm shocked to see Tom standing outside a classroom, and my heart all but stops. He's wearing a black waistcoat today over a charcoal-grey shirt, and it physically hurts to look at him.

To my surprise, he takes two steps towards me.

"They don't have anything on us. There's no evidence. This is just a rumour," he says, quickly and quietly.

"How do you know?" I whisper back, looking around to check the corridor is still empty. It is.

"I'd have heard something by now. I'm listening to everyone's thoughts. There's nothing. It's just hot gossip."

Relief floods my body. Could this be true? Could he be right? God, I hope so.

We stare at each other, a moment suspended in time. He looks tired and wary, but okay. As frustratingly handsome as ever. I must look like a hag, having just indulged in my little loo-based freak-out.

"I have to go," he says.

There's tenderness in his voice, and it warms me.

"Of course," I say, wanting anything but.

He turns quickly on his heel and leaves.

20

We're called in just after lunch on Friday.

"Our investigation concludes that the rumour is unsubstantiated. I'm sorry to have put you both through this," Mr Montgomery announces as soon as we sit down.

Tom flops back in his chair, releasing a sigh of relief. There's a moment of silence as we process the news.

"Did you find out who started the rumour?" Tom asks.

"No, I'm afraid not." Mr Montgomery looks genuinely upset by this.

We both sit motionless, astounded, as though we've both miraculously survived a car crash that should have been fatal.

"Now what?" I ask.

Mr Montgomery makes a movement that could almost be a shrug. "You get on with your lives and put all this behind you. I'm just sorry we couldn't find the culprit."

I daren't look at Tom. My heart is thundering in my chest, and I'm certain he can hear it. Have we done it? Have we somehow got away with this?

We exchange pleasantries for a moment, then Mr Montgomery dismisses us. As we leave, the door clicking closed behind us, Tom turns to me.

"Have a great Christmas, Emilie," he says with the most breathtaking smile on his face.

The urge to grab him and devour his mouth is strong, but I resist.

"And a brilliant New Year," he adds.

"I most certainly will," I reply in a sing-song voice, all but floating down the corridor.

I'm still buoyant with the news as I pack my bags and wish my fellow classmates a happy Christmas. I manage to communicate to Sara, via the subtlest of nods, that we've somehow got through this ordeal unscathed. Everyone starts to leave, and as planned, my parents collect me from outside the school. I hug Sara goodbye. As the car pulls away, I finally relax. Holy shit. We've done it... haven't we?

My parents begin to quiz me about the term just gone. I admire the warm glow of light from the homes in the approaching darkness. The street lights start to come on. Eventually, the questions stop, and Dad puts some music on for the rest of the drive.

It's as I reach into my bag for my lip balm that I feel something unfamiliar. At first I think it's a receipt, but it's too substantial for that. I pull it out and manage, just, to read it in the fading light. It's a note on a sheet of crumpled A4; black, spidery handwriting, scruffy but still legible and in all caps.

END IT WITH MR WAKEFIELD OR I'LL GIVE MONTGOMERY THE EVIDENCE.

Every millilitre of blood drains from my body. I feel as though someone has taken the blade of a scythe and driven it deep into my diaphragm. I think I'm going to be sick, and I mentally assign my handbag as an emergency receptacle.

Fuck.

Fuck, fuck, fuck.

My chest aches. I fleetingly wonder if it's possible to die of a broken heart. Who wrote the note? Who put it in my bag? It doesn't matter now.

This is it, I realise. This is how it ends. I can't meet him now. We're not safe, after all. It was a brilliant lie, a fantasy, an illusion.

It's over.

21

When I was eleven, my mum finally allowed me to walk home from school on my own.

Every day, I would pass a huge red-brick wall, too tall for even the tallest adult to see over. A curious child, I couldn't help but wonder what was behind it and one day, when I was feeling particularly adventurous, I went exploring and found a solid wooden door largely obscured by a hedge. Although the door was locked, I found if I leant on it and shook the janky handle with all the strength my eleven-year-old self could muster, I could get the door to open.

The first time I saw behind that wall, I don't think I took a breath for an entire minute.

I'd stumbled upon a walled garden, full of flowers of every shade, carefully tended lawns crossed with sweeping stone paths. The garden housed a small apple orchard, an ornate birdhouse, a stone statue of a semi-clad Grecian goddess. In the centre stood a captivating glass orb, a water feature, that glowed when the sun caught it. It was like something out of a fairy tale; a slice of paradise, almost too perfect to be true. Almost. Whoever owned this garden, these people, they were hoarding all this beauty for themselves.

Which is how I justified my actions. Every day, on my way home from school, I visited that garden. Lying under the apple trees, watching the blossom falling gently from their boughs and eating the remains of my packed lunch, I'd let my imagination run wild, dreaming up various scenarios in which my fairy princess alter ego would gallop around on her horse and always get the boy.

Sometimes, I'd simply lie on my back in the sunshine with my eyes closed, luxuriate in the warmth and drink up the scent of honeysuckle. When it rained, I'd shelter under the ivory-clad trellis and notice how the perfume of the garden changed.

My mum noticed a difference in me. She didn't seem concerned about the fact that I was at least half an hour late home every day, but she was interested in the change in my demeanour.

"You seem very content, Emilie," she'd said to me one day, a soft smile on her face as she stood at the sink preparing dinner. I didn't know what to say, and I couldn't admit why, so I simply said nothing.

May slid into June; June glided into July. The end of term approached, the summer holidays nearly within reach. I made plans to continue my visits, secretly thrilled in the knowledge that I'd finally have more time to spend there.

I should have known it wouldn't last.

One hot afternoon in July, I entered the garden to find I wasn't alone. Immediately, I knew I was in serious trouble.

The old man was furious. He brandished his secateurs at me, red-faced and bellowing. "You're trespassing, young lady! Get out before I call the police!"

I didn't need to be told twice.

I fled, running home as fast as my little legs could carry me. By the following day, the old lock had been replaced with something infinitely more secure and, just like that, I was never able to visit again.

I still remember the crisp, sweet tang of the orchard's apples. I remember the flowers, the birdsong, my little slice of paradise.

To this day, I miss it still.

22

It's June, a Friday lunchtime. I'm in the SU bar, glass of wine in hand, and this afternoon I have the last exam of my university career. At the risk of sounding ungrateful, I'm so ready for my time here to be over. Final-year burnout is no joke.

I take a long slug of my wine. Who drinks Malbec in the middle of the day? I do, apparently. And I'm certainly not alone in my day drinking, judging by the table of eighteen-year-olds a few feet away. One of them has dark, floppy hair that reminds me of Tom. I watch, waiting, until he turns towards me so I can look at his face. It is, as ever, a disappointment. They always are, an impossible competition, the odds rigged by virtue of the fact they're not the man I was once so deeply in love with.

What's Tom doing now? I wonder. I think this far too often, an overused neural pathway, a groove I can't seem to dislodge myself from. Does he think of me? Does he have a new life? A wife? Kids, perhaps? Even at night, my brain doesn't let up. With a regularity I find disturbing, I wake from dreams where I've turned up at his school all these years later and, in front of a classroom full of kids, I declare my love for him in some dramatic and irresponsible gesture. But I never get to see his response. I always wake, sobbing, as I'm telling him I made a terrible mistake.

No one here knows me from college as I'd feared. I still carry our relationship with me, a devastating injury that healed all wrong. It pulls when I move, a wound sewn too tight, skin with no give left. Truthfully, I was certain I'd feel different by now but, perversely, the lacklustre relationships and awkward sexual encounters I embarked on in a bid to erase Tom from my heart have had the opposite effect. I've been frustrated by every man I date, their relative lack of empathy and warmth, the marked absence of affection and their feeble, inadequate fumblings. I know I only have myself to blame, that I'm probably being too picky. Perhaps I'm subconsciously selecting the wrong men as some kind of masochistic punishment.

I never met Tom in the New Year – how could I? But I did do something spectacularly stupid: I wore clothes I knew he wouldn't recognise me in, some oversized sunglasses and a brunette wig and stood a safe distance from the café we'd agreed to meet at.

Oh, how I stared, as if trying to burn the image of him onto my retinas. He looked so relaxed, sat sipping his coffee, seemingly confident I would show. In my hoodie pocket I held on to the anonymous note as a solid, physical reminder as to why I couldn't possibly go inside.

I can't tell you how long I stood there. When I finally re-entered my body, I realised how laboured my breathing had become. And my face was suddenly wet, tears pooling beneath my sunglasses. I'd expected to feel something, the usual desperate pull towards him, but I hadn't expected the raw, unpalatable anguish, to feel my heart shatter all over again. I didn't anticipate how much it would break me.

Returning home from this spectacularly bad decision, I'd had to feign burnout, the flu, exhaustion. My parents were concerned, bless them, but it was all I could do to remember to breathe, to put one foot in front of the other, to force a pathetic amount of food down my throat. I didn't have the energy to reassure them.

It was a relief to escape to university months later, to be away from the hushed conversations about me they didn't realise I could overhear, to no longer be under such close scrutiny. I've already decided that when I'm done here, with my exams, I won't be returning home. Truthfully, I don't know what to do next with my life; I was absolutely certain I would know by now. I can't stomach the thought of dealing with my parents' relentless if well-intentioned questions.

I'm taking another sip of my wine, savouring the sour, blackcurrant taste, when my phone rings. I reach into my bag, expecting it to be a housemate or my landlord, so I'm shocked to see it's Sara. How odd. We kept in touch after college, but our contact's now dwindled to lengthy bi-monthly WhatsApp updates. She never calls me.

"Hello?"

"Hey! Emilie! How are you?"

"I'm... good. Yeah."

"Try to sound more convincing next time, eh?"

I laugh. It's like no time has passed since we were at college together. "Sorry. I've never been a great liar – you know that."

She snorts at this. "Listen, you know phone calls give me the ick, so I'll keep this short. I'm having an end-of-exams drinks thingy. A pub crawl in Brighton. Last weekend in July. Please say you'll come."

This catches me off guard, and I try to buy myself more time. "Oh, end of July you say?"

"Yup. It'll mostly be my uni mates and a handful of people from college."

"Oh okay, cool."

"C'mon – please come. We've not seen each other in ages. We can get pissed on the beach and stay in a dingy seaside hotel afterwards."

"You're really selling it."

"Please, Emilie. I miss you."

It's her sincerity, the genuine feeling in her voice, that really gets me in my cold, loveless heart. Damn it.

"Okay. I'll come," I find myself saying. "Message me the deets."

I can hear her vibrating with excitement on the other end of the line. "You won't regret it," she buzzes.

23

If I'm honest, I find Brighton obnoxious – the pumped-up motorbikes that insist on circling the town, the pavements heaving with people, many of whom seem alarmingly drunk given it's still light. My stomach rumbles as I stride past restaurants, the enticing scent of food hanging in the air. Brighton, I think, is for extroverts. Give me a quiet rural pub any day of the week.

I have to push past a preoccupied hen do to get inside the trendy bar we'd agreed to meet at. I'm so relieved when I walk through the door and spot Sara immediately.

"Emilie!" she yells, giving precisely zero fucks about everyone else's eardrums. She elbows her way through the crowd and embraces me unapologetically. "I'm so glad you came."

"Me too," I say, and realise I actually mean it. It's great to see her again.

"Let me get you a drink," she insists.

I know better than to argue. She orders me a cocktail, which tells me everything I need to know about how this evening will likely pan out.

We return to the table Sara's secured, and she introduces me to eight women I've never met before and whose names I forget immediately.

"So what are you planning to do with your summer then, Sar?" I ask, taking a sip of the espresso martini I know I'll regret later. Her last WhatsApp update was mostly exam angst and existential dread.

"I've been offered a job," she replies, raising her voice so I can hear her above the general din. "An apprenticeship. Designing wedding dresses."

My mouth drops open. This news is both shocking and entirely unsurprising at the same time. "You're not going to pursue medicine?" Her parents had desperately wanted Sara to use her magic in a hospital setting.

She shakes her head, beaming. "No. My parents are livid."

"I can imagine."

"It was a happy accident – right place, right time. I ended up working in a bridal shop around my studies to earn some extra cash, and the rest just fell into place."

I think back to our manifestation classes and wonder if the future Sara had been sunbathing in was in fact entirely unrelated to medicine.

"I'll be studying alongside the job for a bit – fashion design – but after that they'll let me loose on the dresses."

"That's amazing!" She looks so happy. This is absolutely the right choice for her, and I'm dismayed to feel a stab of envy in the face of such clarity. I'm a bad friend. Just a human friend, but still.

"What about you? What's the plan now?"

"I... don't know yet. Still figuring it out." Turns out there's not a plethora of jobs lined up for philosophy graduates. I was a fool for not specialising; crippled by indecision, I couldn't decide upon an area of magic to pursue and instead ended up doing a generic non-magic degree.

She leans towards me, eyes shining. "You know, I've been stalking you on social media. Your photos are stunning – you could do something with that."

I joined just about every club I could when I first started university. Photography and running club were the only two I actually stuck with.

"Wedding photographers are in high demand," she continues. "And I'll need a photographer to take pictures of my creations. Not to mention, we're always looking for models."

This idea settles in my brain like a seed. But before I can contemplate further, we're interrupted by a sudden squeal. I look up to see that a clumsy passer-by has spilt half his pint over one of Sara's friends.

"Oh shit! Are you okay?" Sara asks.

She looks understandably grumpy. "Sticky," she says, pulling a face.

"Shall we go sit outside?" Sara offers. "There might be more space out there."

There are no free tables outside, and we have to loiter for ages until a group finally leaves. It's at least marginally quieter out here, though, so conversation can be had more easily.

Someone orders another round of drinks, and I find myself holding something pink and overly sweet as we finally make ourselves at home on a huge wooden picnic bench.

As she moves to sit down, I finally notice what Sara is wearing. It suits her perfectly.

"Great outfit," I coo.

"Thanks," she replies. I notice she doesn't return the compliment, and I don't blame her. I opted for an unimaginative black body-con dress. It's underwhelming at best.

My next drink, when it arrives, is a suspicious neon ombre concoction. I make a mental note to get the next round, not least so I can order myself something less reminiscent of toxic waste.

As the night wears on, I already know I won't remember much of it tomorrow, fuzzy-headed as I am with alcohol and disinterest. But I'm jarred awake when half of the group goes to the loo en masse and Sara moves to sit next to me again.

"I still think about that fucking note, you know. Did you ever find out who it was?"

I sober up quickly. "No, don't be daft. You'd have been the first to know."

She shakes her head, looking over at the beach. "Fucking tragedy, that whole situation. You'd have made a great couple."

Even now, it hurts to hear those words.

She turns to look at me. "Let me get you another drink," she says carefully.

I guess the expression on my face must say it all.

We move to another venue, this one dimly lit and throbbing with music. I'm handed another drink – in this light, I can't even see what colour it is. We inch our way towards the heaving dance floor and grind our bodies inappropriately against one of the industrial-looking pillars. It's so humid in here, and I'm contemplating how to escape when I spot her just two feet away. Recognition is instant; she hasn't changed a bit.

"Oh my God! Emilie!" Her voice is a foghorn that cuts effortlessly through the music.

"Becky. Wow. What brings you to Brighton?"

She jabs a finger in the direction of a woman standing with her back to the wall. She looks supremely awkward.

"Birthday drinks!" she blasts.

I nod. Well, well. What are the chances of that?

"You?" she asks.

"Post-exam drinks."

Sara suddenly appears by my side. "Becky! Fancy seeing you here."

Despite the sheer volume of alcohol she's consumed, Sara must have noticed my unease and come to my rescue.

"Wanna get some air?" she all but shouts into my ear.

I nod. But my heart sinks as Becky hands her drink to her friend and follows on behind us. Damn.

We keep walking until we're on the beach. The breeze is a balm, a far cry from the hothouse we've just come from. We gather on the shingle, the glitzy lights of the pier reflecting off the water. The sky is a pale purple. It'll be light soon.

"So what are you up to these days?" Sara prompts.

I wonder if she's actually interested or whether she's just much better than me at making small talk.

"I was working in a garden centre. Handed in my notice last week."

Sara makes polite noises before one of her other friends grabs her by the arm and drags her away to talk to someone else. My heart sinks. I'm not sure I can do this. I'm too drunk for small talk.

"So... it's been a while since college," I try. A diabolical attempt, truly.

"Yeah."

"Do you miss it?" At this point, I'd genuinely be glad if someone knocked me unconscious and dragged me away.

She snorts. "No. Do you?"

"Er. No." At this point, I can hardly say otherwise, and I don't have a neat answer to that question. My college days were... complicated.

"I missed Mr Wakefield when he left, though," she says with a lewd sneer.

I try to keep it light. "Yeah, I think most of the school did."

Suddenly, Becky makes direct eye contact with me. "I have a confession to make," she says, pretending to hang her head in shame like a naughty puppy who peed on her mum's favourite rug. She pauses for added drama. "I put that note in your bag."

It's the way she tells me this, like a punchline to a joke, as though she's recounting something her badly behaved nephew did. Not something *she* did, in very recent history.

"I knew there couldn't be anything going on," she continues. "But I couldn't resist pranking you. Mr Wakefield was hot, wasn't he?"

She suddenly looks concerned. "Are you okay?"

I realise the cause of her concern; I appear to be swaying.

"Sorry, just really drunk," I lie. "I'll be okay." Also a lie.

"You're not angry, are you?" Her tone borders on indignant, like that would be inappropriate. "It was just a prank."

I shake my head, realising the importance of this moment. I imagine turning my emotions off as though there's a big switch in my brain for that very purpose.

"No, it's fine. It was nothing, really. Just a silly rumour."

"Talking of hot men, I'm off to Australia next month to move in with mine. My fiancé, that is."

This revelation jolts me. She looks unbearably smug, holding up her left hand to showcase a frankly gaudy ring. It's not the engagement I care about, though.

"Australia?" I try to hide my incredulity.

"Yeah. I'm hoping to get married in the summer. Christmastime."

"Oh, right. Wow." There's a beat, a pause that's too long, my brain still processing what she's said. She didn't know about us. The note was "just" a prank. And she's moving to the other side of the world next month.

"Congratulations," I manage, so preoccupied with all the thoughts now firing in my brain that I can barely see what's in front of my face.

"Thanks." She's wearing a horribly gleeful expression. It hits me, suddenly. I can't be here anymore.

"Sorry, excuse me…" I say, and I turn and walk away.

The sun is starting to come up, the sky growing lighter. I find the edge of the water and remove my shoes so that my aching feet make contact with wet sand. There are a handful of random stragglers sitting on the shingle, some still drinking, here presumably to watch the sunrise.

After all this time, it was Becky. It was "just" a harmless teenage prank. One that destroyed my life.

I inch into the sea so that the water laps at my ankles. It is, to my surprise, not nearly as cold as I thought it would be.

I feel spinny and off-centre, but it's not the alcohol. The filter through which I'd been seeing my life play out has been replaced with something completely different. I'm weightless, disoriented. A woman groping in the dark for a light switch.

I throw my shoes and bag behind me, and start to wade deeper into the water. It soothes my aching feet, and I fantasise about going all the way in, washing my skin, which is sticky with sweat and spilt cocktails.

There was no evidence. She didn't even believe the rumour. The note was just entertainment to her. Unwitting devastation, born of boredom. And this woman, the cause of so much heartache, is moving to Australia next month.

I inch further in, the water now at mid-thigh. I can feel the buoyancy of it pushing me back up. I wonder if this is what it feels like to walk on the moon.

My brain wrestles with this new information, still trying to assimilate: there was never any evidence, just a rumour. Perhaps Becky started that, but I imagine she would've admitted to that too if so.

Fuck it. I'm doing it, consequences be damned. I launch forward, diving into the water. When I surface, I flip so I can lie on my back.

I know I must look unhinged, but it feels so good. My scalp prickles as the cold water comes into contact with my head. There's something about floating in the sea like this that makes me feel totally insignificant, but in a good way. Like my life is both utterly inconsequential but also that I'm a microscopic part of something bigger—

"EMILIE!"

Uh-oh. It's Sara's voice that reaches me from across the waves, her anger unmistakable.

"What in the LIVING FUCK are you DOING?"

24

In my pyjamas and wearing Sara's dressing gown, wet hair wrapped in a towel, I follow my friend out onto our room's tiny balcony and sit at a rickety wrought-iron table that's seen better days.

"You promise me it wasn't some cry for help?" she says, handing me a glass of water.

"Jesus Christ, Sar. No. I realise how it looked, but... no. I was just hot."

Sara takes a sip of her own water. "You scared me."

"I'm really sorry."

"Was making small talk with Becky really that bad?"

"Well..." I trail off. When I say the words, I can't believe they're coming out of my mouth. "I found out who put that note in my bag at the end of term..."

Sara's eyes widen, and her mouth forms a perfect "O".

"It was Becky," I finish.

"WHAT?" The word fires out of her like a bullet.

"Yup."

"Fucking hell! So after all this time, it was her? What did she say?"

"Just that it was a harmless teenage prank. She didn't actually have any evidence; she didn't even believe the rumour. She thought she was being funny. Oh, and she's leaving the country next month."

Sara is gripping the edge of the wrought-iron table, the tips of her fingers white. "That bitch. Honestly. She's always been jealous of you, of your talent and academic prowess. She struggled at school, didn't she? Always getting into trouble, always fucking up her magic. She says it was just a prank, but it was interesting she chose you, wasn't it? There's got to be a reason for that."

"I guess it doesn't matter now."

"True. All that matters now is what you do with this information." Sara shakes her head. "I don't think it was any coincidence we saw her tonight. I'd put money on her having seen my invite online and figuring she'd invite herself along."

"That sounds like something Becky would do."

Sara's face changes, her expression suddenly the most intense I've ever seen it. "You're going to go and find him, right? Hunt him down and explain everything?"

"Sar, it's not that simple."

"Why the fuck not? Are you mad?"

"It's been years."

She gives me a look. "You're not going to get closure unless you try to find him."

"He'll surely have a girlfriend or wife by now. And/or kids; there's no way he's single. Not to mention, he could be anywhere. It's not like I have his number."

I'm sure I've caught her out, that I've made such a compelling and obvious case that she'll have no comeback. I should have known better.

"So you're just not going to bother then?" She throws her arms up in the air to underline her point. "You'll just continue to be tormented by what might have been. How's that working out for you?"

Shit. She's right, of course. That torment has had its claws in me since Tom and I parted ways.

When I say nothing, Sara carries on. "You must go and find him, Emilie. You realise what this means, right? You can pursue that relationship with wild abandon. You're safe, now."

Those words – a ten-tonne realisation – smack me right in the heart.

I'm safe now.

Finally.

And so is he.

I'm usually one of those irritating morning people incapable of sleeping past 6 a.m., but the following day I sleep in and wake just after 10 a.m., ravenously hungry. Sara is already awake and dressed, mumbling something about being grateful for having booked a late checkout. I struggle to imagine she's slept.

She narrows her eyes at me. "You look better today despite last night's cocktails and scant sleep. How are you feeling?"

I take a moment to check in with myself. "Surprisingly good. Have you eaten?"

"Nope. Figured we'd grab food as soon as you woke up."

I slowly extricate myself from the bed and wander over to the mirror to assess the damage. Sara is rummaging around in her suitcase, muttering something about crossover colours.

"Try this. It's clean," she says, throwing a cornflower-blue dress at me.

I hold it up against myself and notice that it mysteriously seems to match my eyes.

She looks smug. "What have I told you about black? Now get in the shower, will you? I'm starving."

I wash in record time, and we head to a nearby café where most of the girls from last night are waiting for us. All looking very much the worse for wear.

"Where's Amelia?" Sara asks.

One of the girls – Livvy, I think? – shakes her head. "She paid for another night at the hotel. She won't be joining us today."

"Ah. Bless."

We make small talk about hangovers and tactical chunders until the food arrives. Poached eggs on avocado toast is exactly what I need today, and I wolf my food down with unbridled abandon to envious looks from others.

"I can't face food yet," Livvy says as she gingerly sips on her black coffee.

The group nods sympathetically.

Sara leans in towards me, that intense expression on her face again. "So what's the plan?" she asks, her voice low so the others can't easily hear us.

"Eat food, get the train home..."

"Emilie."

"Sorry. I don't know. I guess I'll have to go to his school? He might not be there anymore, but it's the only lead I have."

She looked satisfied and nods. "Yes. That's what you'll do. Keep me posted, okay? I want twice-hourly updates from here on in."

After brunch, Sara hugs her way around the group as she says her goodbyes. I realise I should get going, too, when she catches my arm.

"Let me call in a favour. Please. No offence, but when was the last time you had a haircut?"

I'm not even offended. "I can't remember."

"I suppose I should just be glad you didn't do anything mad like dye it black."

I did, actually, in my first year of university. It went horribly, horribly wrong, and I had to pay an obscene amount of money to an unsympathetic hairdresser to fix it. But Sara doesn't need to know about that.

The hairdresser – Nancy – is known for her hairdressing wizardry, and I feel safe in her competent hands. She works in silence, focused solely on the task in hand, and I fall into a trance as she moves around me, making thoughtful noises. I feel incredibly calm, and I notice this because it's new for me. These last few years haven't just been full of heartache, I realise. I haven't just been grieving my relationship with Tom. My days have been full of an ever-present undercurrent of anxiety that comes, unsurprisingly, from being blackmailed. Believing that someone out there had evidence that could destroy Tom's life (and mine, to a lesser degree) whenever the fancy took them. It was all just an illusion, a lie, but I had no way of knowing that.

There's another feeling in the mix, too, I realise: clarity. For the first time in years, I finally know what to do next.

Eventually, Nancy stops and looks at me. "All done," she says, whipping her hairdresser's cape away like a stage magician.

I'd been so preoccupied with my thoughts that I hadn't even noticed she'd finished. I look up and eye myself in the mirror. "Wow."

Nancy nods. "Sara's a clever woman. She knew exactly what your face shape needed."

I look like I've been given a facelift. How is that even possible? In fact, paired with Sara's cornflower-blue dress, all those years of heavy drinking have somehow been erased from my face.

Sara rises from the chair she's been waiting patiently on and stands beside me, resting a hand on my shoulder, like a wise fairy godmother.

"Ah, yes…" she says, looking deservedly smug. "That'll do nicely."

25

After a long and uneventful train journey, I arrive home late in the evening and crash into bed. The following day, I wake and begin my investigations immediately, starting with the school Tom told me he was moving to. I search online and find the website, but there's no list of staff as I'd assumed there would be. Which leaves me with no choice – I'll have to drive to the school and try to track him down. The thought makes me immediately uneasy; I imagine myself walking around the school, peering through classroom windows, getting escorted off the grounds before I even get a glimpse of him. But what else can I do? It's the only information I have.

    I drive for hours, stopping only when absolutely necessary. When I arrive, it's three o'clock in the afternoon – kicking-out time. The school gates are open to allow everyone to leave. Do I slip in now to see if I can find him? Or loiter outside and wait for him to leave? I decide to wait, afraid of being caught. I'm fairly certain there's only one entrance and exit from this school, and I wait a few metres from it.

It's unseasonably cold, and my clothing is woefully inadequate for this unexpected drop in temperature. I pace the pavement, trying to warm myself up.

Two hours later, just when I'm starting to believe I might be the first person in history to develop hypothermia in July, I see him leave the main building and walk towards the car park. I run-walk in his direction then slow as I near him. He looks up as I approach, and our eyes meet. The shock of seeing him again is physical.

"Emilie," he says, breathless. Somehow, it sounds as though my name has been punched out of him.

"I don't want to talk here." I gesture to the school. "Will you meet with me?"

He looks like he's seen a ghost. "Yes."

"Okay," I say. And then we just stand there, staring at each other. I feel his gaze on every inch of me, analysing me; my clothes, my face, the bag I'm holding. I wonder if I look older, wiser, more jaded. I certainly feel it.

I study him, a visual feast: same crisp white shirt and thin black tie. His hair is a bit shorter. My gaze darts to his hands. No wedding ring.

Neither of us says a word; we just stare at each other. After the longest silence I've ever experienced in my twenty-one years, I realise I need to give this man a time and place to meet, so I do. And then I turn on my heel and leave before I can say anything else.

26

We meet at a pub I drove past en route to Tom's school. Although it looked pretty from the outside, as soon as I get inside, I realise I've made a terrible mistake. It's dark and grimy, and completely empty. There's no music playing in the background, which means that the creepy bartender will be able to overhear every word we say.

Tom arrives only a minute after me. He's changed out of his school clothes into some jeans and a dark navy check shirt, and my entire body responds. I have to make a conscious effort to control my breathing. He is, impossibly, even more attractive than I remember.

"Can I get you a drink?" I offer, remembering I was the one that invited him here.

He seems surprised by this, even though we're literally in a pub where drinking is the expected activity.

"Oh. Sure. Thank you. I'll have the Fentimans cola."

I wonder if he's ordering it for the caffeine. I order the same. Out of sight of Tom, the creepy bartender literally looks me up and down, and I swear I see him lick his lips. Gross. No wonder the place is empty if he's perving on the clientele.

I return to our seats with the drinks. My hands are shaking, and cola drips onto the shiny black table. I arrange myself in the seat opposite, my heart fluttering in my chest. I can't read Tom's expression. He's waiting for me to speak. In my single-mindedness, I didn't stop to consider what I might actually *say* to him.

He looks at me, expectant, and my tongue, now mysteriously bone dry, sticks to the roof of my mouth. I take a sip of my cola and then speak.

"I was terrified you'd go to prison."

I could have started with small talk, the how are yous, but that felt somehow disingenuous.

"I know," he says softly. There's a long pause before he speaks again. "I should have waited. I should have exercised self-control. I was blinded by my feelings for you."

I'm momentarily winded, hearing him talk about his feelings for me. Does he still feel that way? Or does he have a new girlfriend – a new life – now?

He doesn't answer these questions, and nothing about his demeanour suggests he's heard them. I can only assume he's blocking my thoughts.

"I'm sorry," I say. "I'm sorry for pursuing you so doggedly. I made your life very difficult."

He's silent, his gaze disconcertingly direct. I blunder on.

"And I'm sorry I had to ghost you."

I see the subtlest change in his expression; a tightening, a tension. His silence is unnerving.

"But you have to understand, Tom: I was blackmailed." I pull the note from my pocket. After all these years, I finally understand why I kept it. I hand it to him, and he takes it, studying it in silence for several seconds.

"Fucking hell." His voice is very quiet, I assume to keep the bartender from overhearing. His face is pale, his knuckles white. "When were you given this?"

"On the Friday before Christmas. I found it in my bag as I was travelling home."

"Who wrote it? Do you know?"

"It was Becky. I only found that out two days ago."

He takes in a big lungful of air. He's clearly wrestling with himself. "And this is why you didn't meet me at the café as planned?"

"Of course it is. Do you really think I would have dared risk it? I couldn't."

"Fucking hell," he says again. He puts his head in his hands, his palms covering his eyes. When he looks at me again, he seems dazed.

"Did she start the rumour?"

"I have no idea. I feel like she would have told me if she had, though. What she did tell me is that she's moving to Australia next month, to start a new life with her fiancé."

Tom sits back in his chair, both hands resting on the table in front of him. I follow his gaze as it darts to the bar. The creepy bartender is doing a terrible job of pretending he isn't listening to our every word.

Tom rolls his eyes and then gets to his feet. "Come on, Emilie. Let's get out of here."

Outside, it's a beautiful summer's evening, much warmer now than it felt earlier. Tom motions to a bridle path beside the pub, and we start to walk down it. The scene before us is quintessentially English – rolling fields, fluffy sheep, red brick farmhouses in the distance.

Tom is quiet for a long time. Eventually, he speaks. "Did you come far today?"

I think about the journey I've made, how long it'll take me to drive back.

"I drove down from Edinburgh."

"That's a long way. Where are you staying tonight?"

"Not sure yet. Hopefully I can find a cheap hotel. If I can't, I'll mainline caffeine and drive back."

The change in his expression is subtle, but I do see him wince.

"It's a long way back."

We walk on, our pace slow and unhurried. He knows about Becky now, about the blackmail. About why I never met him at the café. An unspoken question hangs in the air. I wonder if he can hear it. I try to focus on our surroundings. With fewer hills, the skies down here seem bigger.

"This whole time…" he says, and then shakes his head. He's struggling to assimilate it, much like I did.

"This whole time you thought I got cold feet."

"I did."

"And this whole time I believed that if I'd met you in that café, there would have been catastrophic consequences for us both. But especially for you."

He nods, his gaze on the uneven path in front of us. He's quiet for ages.

"Fuck," he says finally.

"It feels like a punishment, doesn't it?"

"It does. It really does."

"Was our relationship so wrong?"

He turns to look out over the fields, shaking his head. "My conscience is clean," he says quietly. Then he motions to a second, smaller track that leads us off the bridle path and into a small, wooded glade. I immediately notice the beautiful golden light, the way it filters through the trees. There's a sign that says "Private Wood".

"Do you worry that, like it or not, the appeal, the reason we were together in the first place, was because I was a student?" I ask.

He shakes his head vehemently. "No. I mean, I enjoyed those fantasies, but..." He sighs. "I really did enjoy those fantasises..." He looks pained by this. "But it wasn't the teacher–pupil dynamic that did it for me. Or even the incredible sex. It was you."

I'm shaking. The birds are singing; melodic chirps and trills fill the air. It's cooler in the shade beneath the trees. I move so that a slice of sunlight warms my back.

"And, God..." He looks away, seeming to study our surroundings before continuing. "I don't know, what's the harm in playing out those fantasies in private? As two consenting, responsible adults who no longer have any legal or moral ramifications hanging over them?"

His words hang in the air. I stand stock-still, winded.

Is he implying what I think he's implying?

"Girlfriend?" I manage, breathing difficult now.

A half-laugh escapes his lips. He shakes his head. "Absolutely not."

He's a couple of metres away and looking directly at me, wearing a long-ago, once-familiar expression. My heart squeezes in my chest.

I take a tentative step towards him, and his face immediately softens.

He exhales. "I never stopped loving you."

27

We're a metre apart now. The rest of the world seems to fall away. I think I might be panting. He takes a step towards me, closing the gap but still keeping a respectful distance. I could reach out and touch him, but I don't.

"You didn't stop?"

He shakes his head.

"But aren't you afraid we've changed? That we've grown apart? That we want different things after all this time?" I realise I'm trembling. He's inches from me.

He sighs. "No."

I'm poised, practically on tiptoes, my body leaning towards him like a tree bending in the wind.

"Emilie, come here."

I close the gap.

His face relaxes as I enter his personal space, as if he's relieved I'm there. I study his dark eyes, the gold-amber halo around his pupils. He smells exactly the same, and my body responds, recognising him and remembering: the furtive exchanges, the filthy fantasies, forbidden fucking in classrooms, gentle lovemaking, the white-hot emotional intensity of it all.

His expression has changed. There's a knowing now, a confidence. I'm teetering on the edge, my mouth inching closer to his.

"Go stand by the oak tree, facing it," he whispers.

Although it sounds like an order, I know it's an invitation. It's how we play the game; how we've always played it. But I don't comply immediately.

"Facing it?"

"Yes. Put your hands and body against the trunk."

I pick my way across the forest floor, legs trembling. I feel clumsy and awkward, and I don't care. I do as instructed, putting my hands on the rough bark and inching closer so my body is leaning against it. I hear the rustle of leaves behind me and I know not to turn around. I feel him, instead, the heat of his body as he stands little more than an inch from me. He rests his hand on the trunk, near mine. I can hear his breathing. It's heavy, like mine. In the relative quiet, with neither of us daring to move, my mind anticipates what might happen next.

I'm wearing a short skirt. It would be easy for him to reach up and pull my knickers down, thrust into me, take me against the rough bark.

But he doesn't. Instead, I feel him gradually press his weight against me so I'm sandwiched tightly between him and the tree.

I let out a moan at the relief of his body finally against mine after so long, the last piece of the jigsaw puzzle sliding into place.

His hand is on my waist, seeking, until he finds a way in beneath my top. Skin on skin, his hand creeps up to my ribcage, across my stomach. He pauses to stroke the soft skin beneath my waistband, the vulnerable underside of my belly.

"Emilie," he mumbles softly, his lips hovering close to my neck. I'm desperate for him to kiss me.

I'm pinned tightly against this tree, his erection jutting into my left buttock. I half-heartedly squirm beneath him, trying to adjust the angle, but he won't allow it. He has me trapped.

His hand inches up towards my bra to undo it, then he slides his fingers underneath so they finally come into contact with my breast.

He gently pinches my nipple, and I cry out.

"Shhh – we shouldn't be here," he murmurs into my neck, but even to my ears, his protest seems half-hearted. He's right, though. I glance around nervously. Thankfully, no one is nearby.

He begins to kiss my neck, so lightly. It's the tenderness with which he does it that makes my legs turn to jelly, and I'm grateful to be sandwiched between Tom and this old oak tree.

"I can't begin to describe how much I've missed you, Emilie," he says, his hand now stroking my hip. I hear the crack in his voice, and I feel the last three years fall away. I have very little idea how he's spent our time apart, but I can't shake the feeling that it doesn't matter.

He relaxes his weight on me a fraction, just enough that he can move his hand under the elastic of my knickers, his fingers just above my pubic bone.

Finally, he eases my underwear down and pushes himself inside me. I cry out in relief, turned on beyond any reasonable measure at the sheer thrill of it. We absolutely shouldn't be here, in this private wood, doing this. I should be terrified, and whilst I am, I'm also relieved because I don't want a sanitised version of what we once had.

He doesn't move very much, just uses his weight to push himself inside me as deeply as he possibly can.

"Fuck. Oh my God, Emilie. Fuck."

"More," I pant.

He eases his weight off me just a fraction and snakes his hand down from my hip into my knickers. His fingers find my slippery clit and, so very slowly, he begins to caress it, his touch feather-light.

I dig my fingers into the bark, my legs starting to tremble as he continues to tease me with lazy, circular movements. I'm tantalisingly close. He pulls back slightly, and I feel his thickness. He moans, his fingers pausing their torment. I arch my back, desperate. I want him to pin me against the tree again, filling me up, touching me so that I come on his big, thick cock.

"Being able to hear your thoughts, Emilie..." he whispers, his warm breath tickling my ear. "There's nothing sexier."

He pushes back inside me, as deep as he can, and his fingers resume their teasing.

"I wish I could hear yours," I manage.

His fingers still in response to this, and he begins to kiss my neck.

"I'm thinking this has to be the best dream I've ever had, that it can't possibly be real," he says, somehow managing to speak between kisses. "How I've missed the noises you make when I'm inside you, the way you tighten around me. And I'm thinking about how badly I want to see the expression on your face when you come."

I manage only a whimper in response, his words turning my blood to fire. I turn my face towards him, and he kisses my hot, flushed cheek before returning his attention to my neck.

His fingers begin to move again, his touch just a fraction too soft. I know this is intentional.

"Please," I beg.

But then I feel Tom tense.

"I thought I saw something," he whispers, and I try not to panic.

We both scan our surroundings, searching the gaps between the trees. It's fine; there's nothing to see within eyeshot, but it's clear our time here has come to an end.

I dig my fingers into the tree in frustration, knowing what's coming. Tom carefully withdraws, and I hear him zip and fasten his jeans. Still facing away from him, I make myself presentable.

"It'll be better if we wait," he promises, sensing my frustration. I'm literally trembling with need.

I turn to face him. His cheeks are flushed, too, hair mussed, his shirt not as straight as before. There's a weighted pause before he speaks.

"Do you want to come back to mine?" he asks. The look on his face is close to desperation.

Do I want to go back to his house?

You fucking bet I do.

"Yes," I utter, barely able to get the word out.

After all this time, after all these years, as if the answer would be anything else.

28

It's nothing short of a miracle that we weren't spotted taking such a risk. On our return to Tom's car we survey the area, checking for people, pets, animals, but there's nothing.

He has the same car he did when we went to Scotland years ago. Smart, black, clean. I sink into the passenger seat, and he starts to drive. Neither of us speak. I'm mute with the enormity of it all.

And I'm so painfully aware of his presence beside me. So I'm not openly gawping at him, I study him from the corner of my eye, looking for differences, but there are none. Instead, I notice his lovely hands, the way he drives so smoothly, the way the corner of his mouth keeps twitching up into a little smile.

He reverses onto his drive, which I think nothing of. I notice we're a little further out of town, the countryside visible. The outskirts of Bath; an enviable location.

I climb out of the car, turn around and nearly lose my fucking mind.

"It's my cottage!" I splutter. "The one from my daydreams!" I have to lean on the car to support myself.

He laughs. "Yes, it is." He walks over to me and slides his arm around my waist as I tremble. "The expression on your face is everything I hoped it would be."

I'm aware I'm doing this weird half-crying, half-panting thing. Attractive.

"Shit. It is *beautiful*."

Holy fucking hell, it is *everything*; sage-green front door, stone walls partially obscured by leafy climbers, white panelled sash windows, a stone pot beside the entrance full of bright blooms. He even has a little wooden table and chairs outside, pot plant in the centre, as if he's been expecting me.

"When did you buy this?" I'm still panting, my body fully shaking now. I'm literally having a breakdown.

He squeezes me tighter against him, which helps.

"About a year into my new teaching job. I've spent the last two years renovating it. It's not quite finished; I've got the study and back garden still to do."

And that's when it hits me like a freight train.

He never stopped loving me.

Not just an overused turn of phrase, a cliché. This, right here, right in front of my very eyes, is the brick-and-mortar proof.

"I never could give up on the idea of us. I hoped you'd come back to me one day." He smiles ruefully, looking a bit embarrassed. "And if you didn't... well, there's worse places to live. And renovating it gave me something to focus on."

I say nothing. I can't. I'm stunned by the beauty of it and what it means.

"Do you want to come inside? Sit down?" he asks. His expression is gently amused.

"Please," I wheeze.

We take it slowly, step by step. I cling to him, my legs jelly. In a stupor, I watch him unlock the front door and we enter. I take in the bare wood floors, the white walls and light oak furniture. He leads me into the lounge, and I nearly implode when I spot the white log burner.

He helps me onto the sofa like a little old woman. My breathing is so laboured now I'm worried I might pass out. He kneels in front of me and takes both of my hands in his.

"Can you breathe a little slower?"

I nod, making a conscious effort to do so. He breathes with me, and I can't help but study my surroundings – tasteful beige sofas, check throw cushions, carefully curated botanical prints that perfectly coordinate with everything else. Honestly, it looks like a fucking interior designer lives here.

"Did you do all this yourself?" I pant.

He simply nods, not taking his eyes off me. "Your breathing, remember?" His smile is gentle.

I refocus on my breath, feeling a big fat salty tear drip down my face and off my cheek. So this is what it's like to live your dream.

"Tea?" he offers. "Would that help?"

"It would," I croak.

Whilst I'm tempted to follow him out to the kitchen so I can ogle some more, I don't trust my legs right now. So I remain seated, listening to the sounds of him moving about next door.

He brings the tea out, a sweet smile on his face. Jesus, even the mug is perfect. A ceramic handmade thing of beauty, not some mass-manufactured mug from a supermarket. I could actually cry.

I sip the tea. It's sweet and comforting and exactly what I need.

"So good," I sigh.

"I'm glad."

He takes a seat opposite me, leaning forward on his knees. "So tell me about the last few years."

I take another sip and shrug. "It's all very underwhelming. Three years of heavy drinking culminating in a half-arsed philosophy degree, a zero-hours contract and a reliance on the goodwill of friends who are happy for me to sleep on their sofa bed in exchange for a pittance in rent and some housework."

He pulls a face. It's grim – I know it is.

"I haven't really found... anything that excites me, career-wise." I hesitate for just a moment, remembering my conversation with Sara. The photography, maybe. Perhaps she's right – perhaps that could be something. "And the financial instability is difficult," I continue. "But I manage. I'm lucky, really. I'm painting a bleak picture, but it's fine."

"I don't know what I would have done had I not gone into teaching," he says. "I'd have probably ended up in a very similar situation. It's hard, and everything is so expensive now."

I nod.

"Is there anything in particular keeping you in Edinburgh?" he asks.

I think about this. "Only friends, really."

"Do you still talk to Sara?"

"Yes, although it's mostly long distance these days. She's not far from here, actually." I take another sip of tea. "What about you? What did you do in those three years?"

He leans back into the sofa. "I buried myself in teaching and doing this place up. Those two things have been all-consuming."

"I can imagine. And..." It's the obvious question to ask, but I hesitate. "Romantically?"

He laughs out of his nose. "No, Emilie. Jesus, how was I supposed to have a relationship and explain this place? 'I'm renovating it just in case the woman I love comes back to me, but don't worry, I'm fully committed to you.' Anyway, I didn't have time for dating. How about you? Got some boyfriend I need to know about?" His tone is light, teasing.

"Hilarious that you think I'd be here if that were the case. No. I had a series of deeply unsatisfying... flings, I guess you'd call them. Considered celibacy for a moment. In that desperate context, I figured the long drive here was worth a shot."

He laughs. "You? Celibacy?"

I feign offence but quickly crumble, trying to cover my laugh. "Well..." I shrug again, cupping both hands around my mug. "I guess that didn't work out, so here we are." I take another sip of my drink. It's possibly the best cup of tea I've ever tasted.

I glance over at him. He looks thoughtful.

"Is it weird me being here?" I ask.

"Very. I'm worried I'll wake up in a minute."

I smile shyly, and my gaze falls back to the mug I'm holding. I hear Tom get to his feet. He comes and sits beside me.

"I've had a thought," he says, looking very earnest. He slips an arm around my shoulders and starts to stroke my hair.

"You have?"

"Yes. But you should put your tea down first before I tell it to you."

My heart starts to pick up speed. I'm not sure how many more surprises my poor body can handle today.

"How would you feel about... moving in with me?"

"*W-What?*"

"Worst case scenario, it doesn't work and you move out. No harm done."

As much as I don't want to, I start to sob. Not pretty, elegant sobs. Big, heaving, ugly, end-of-the-world sobs.

Do I want to move into the cottage of my literal dreams, with the man I've been missing and longing for these last three years?

"I built most of this place myself, and yet I feel like I'm living in *your* home. It seems peculiar you not being here with me."

"But what if—" I stop. I have nothing.

"Would you miss your friends? I don't want to tear you away from them."

I don't know much, but I do know this: Jenny will be delighted to have her guest room back so her brother and his new baby can finally visit. And, just as importantly, Sara and I would no longer have to endure a crappy long-distance friendship. She's going to flip her actual *shit* when she finds out about this.

I'm still sobbing. I try to control myself so I can make words come out of my mouth.

"I think my friends will be happy to have their spare rooms back," I manage.

He takes my face in his hands. "Is that a yes, then?" He looks on the verge of tears himself, which is easily enough to send me over the edge. The sobs erupt again.

"Oh, Emilie." He laughs, a tear running down his cheek.

"You waited for me," I hiccup.

"I did."

He carefully wipes the tears from my face as my sobs finally start to subside.

"It's a yes?" he tries again.

"It's a yes."

We gaze dumbly at each other. I notice the wet trail on his cheek that his lone tear left in its wake.

"Can I kiss you?" he asks softly.

As if he needs to ask.

It starts off so gentle and toe-curlingly tender, as though I'm something precious to be treasured. But before long, his hands are in my hair, and I'm tugging at his shirt.

"Do you want to see our bedroom?" he asks.

As it happens, I very much do.

Author's note

Thank you, dearest reader, for reading this book. It's thrilling to know that my story made it into your hands, and I hope you had the best time reading it.

I can't overstate how much fun I had writing this novella. It was one of those stories that seemed to fall from the ether; I went to bed one night with the observatory scene in my mind, like a still from a film, and when I woke the story was ready to be written. I staggered from my bed to my desk and wrote the first 7,000 words in five days (still in my PJs) - a record for me!

The story seemed to take on a life of its own, in the way that all the best stories do. It was like being possessed by some benevolent daemon; my laundry piled up, the cat litter went unhoovered, and at one point I ran out of clean knickers. It was a joyous birth, but I'll be the first to admit my personal hygiene took a hit.

I've been writing for as long as I can remember, and over time I've learned that I can't force the words. I've stopped trying to bully myself into writing 2,000 words a day, my creativity simply doesn't respond to that. Instead, I've learned to woo the muse; when I get stuck, I take walks, chat with friends about the story, or indulge in what I call 'quality input' (which, yes, might include bingeing *Love Is Blind* on Netflix). Sometimes I'll switch it up entirely, whether that's singing, or taking my DSLR out for a walk. It all seems to help.

If you want to hear about future releases, learn more about my writing process, or **see some exclusive character art**, join my newsletter at jasmineharperwrites.com. I don't send newsletters often, so you can rest assured I won't be overwhelming your inbox.

With love and immense gratitude,

Jasmine x

About the author

Jasmine Harper is a romance writer from England who loves crafting steamy stories. She draws inspiration from nature – especially the moon and the soft pastel skies at dusk – to infuse emotion and magic into her work. When she's not writing, she's reading tarot for friends, sniffing her cats, or indulging in her guilty pleasure: playing The Sims. Her go-to books for writing wisdom are *Big Magic*, *The Artist's Way*, and *Bird by Bird*.

Check out her work and sign up for updates at jasmineharperwrites.com.

Printed in Great Britain
by Amazon